Surviving the Killzone

By
Cedric Spicer

Cadmus Publishing
www.cadmuspublishing.com

Published by Cadmus Publishing
www.cadmuspublishing.com
Port Angeles, WA

ISBN: 978-1-63751-015-5

Hands off! All rights reserved.

Any violators get a one way ticket to THE KILLZONE!

Author's Note

DEDICATION

For,

Hazel Spicer, may you rest in eternal peace.
Valerie Spicer. I love you Mommy, I did it!!

CONTENTS

PROLOGUE

I love a good hard suck to get things going," Naomi openly confessed. She put a little extra on her walk, making her ass enticingly wiggle as she walked toward her client and offered him her creamy center.

This was out of her normal. Circumstances of the laws changed things. Having a client was foreign, but after last night's events she needed a release.

He smiled and laid back on the bed admiring the beauty before him. She could tell he didn't know or couldn't decide what her nationality was. He kept speaking different languages to see if she responded. Naomi didn't respond even though she understood a couple of them.

"Come here!" he demanded from his back. Naomi grinned. Seductively she walked closer and climbed on the bed. It's been a while since she was here, in this moment. Purposely she let her head bypass his shaft only slightly, brushing it with her nose. His tool tilted as she crawled up his body.

"What are you doing to me, girl?" He inhaled a moan. "Shit!"

She smiled, making it to her desired position. "Ooh, there's nothing better than a guy who knows how to use his tongue." Naomi bit her bottom lip and planted herself on the client's face.

After a good pussy licking, she turned the table and descended upon the client's tool—first with her mouth and then with her soaking, pleading wet juice box.

The sex was intensely in motion. Shockingly, the client actually knew what he was doing, and she enjoyed every second. Naomi wiped the sweat forming on her forehead as she bounced continuously on his tool. She could tell he was feeling himself as well as he up stroked matching her pace.

"TAKE IT! TAKE DIS DICK, BITCH!" he boasted. "How dis dick feel?"

"Ummm, good." She inhaled and exhaled.

Naomi noticed a look of ecstasy on her face as she watched herself in the ceiling mirror. Closing her eyes, she was nearing the big O.

Naomi opened her eyes for a second. She felt a presence other than theirs. "Ugh!" Her face soured.

"What's up?" he asked as he wiped sweat beads from his face.

"That!" Naomi pointed from on top of him, still trying to catch her orgasm as she bounced.

Diamond stood in the doorway and smiled. "Damn, Nay-Nay! Looks like you really enjoying the op. Did I interrupt?" she asked, pointing her pearl handle .380 pistol.

The client pushed Naomi off of him and she fell to the floor had. "What the fuck is goin' on?!" he asked, now standing on the opposite side of the bed.

Naomi was tight. "No, this nigga didn't," she said standing up. The guy threw her hard and she was now in her feelings. She stood ass naked with heels and her hair wild. Give me the gun, bitch!" she demanded, walking toward Diamond with her hand out.

Diamond was hesitant, but Naomi was persistent. Diamond gave in. "Here, don't do nothing stupid."

"Like what?"

Five continuous rounds made the barrel spit fire. Diamond jumped back. "Like that, bitch!" she raised her voice. "You didn't even get the money . . ."

INTRODUCTION

"Did you get the picture yet, I'm painting you a portrait."

— Naomi

The president should have been impeached for even presenting this particular bill into Congress. The Killzone. It was in full effect. Like a power struck kid, the president makes rash decisions on the whelm. Most Washingtonians call him an Aryan, minus a sheet and torch. If this bill wasn't racist, the city must not know the definition of the word.

The laws that were legalized basically are death sentences to all residents living in the Nation's Capital. Heaven can wait while they all watch the skies. Hopes for the best, but likely to receive the worst. Many die young with life expectancy dreams of forever.

Today's date, June 15th. Reality set in. Cruising, a rare way of driving nowadays. A red light neared. Caution and vigilance is a must.

Across the street Naomi noticed a father, her assumption. She watched him. On a park bench he sat all the while placing a gift on a little girl's lap. It was wrapped beautifully. The girl is no older than seven. Her face appeared joyful as the city was dark.

For a slight second Naomi's eyes wandered. The sun was its highest in the sky. The rays felt wonderful on her skin. She felt wonderful just to be alive. The little girl eagerly unwrapped the gift that was covered in pink with a yellow bow, her favorite colors. Naomi had to squint her eyes to make sure they weren't deceiving her as the gift was revealed.

"Wow!" Naomi was puzzled. She clears her mind and then she understands.

In her hand, her tiny hand, she held the handle of a pink and chrome 3.80 handgun. Surprisingly she cocks it with a bright smile, then places the gun into her Dora, the Explorer backpack and happily jumps into her father's embrace.

The light is long. Still red. A car pulled up abruptly stopping in front of the family.

"Oh shit!" Naomi's eyes bubble. Trouble.

The father reached for his weapon and stood in the way of his daughter as he tried to get the drop. He wasn't fast enough. BOOM!!

A single shot knocked the father off his feet. He wasn't moving. The driver of the car stood over top of the father, rolling him over with the heel of his foot. He said something when the father was on his back as he raised his gun to finish the deed. Naomi shook her head from behind the driver's seat knowing what's to come.

Three quick thunderous, but deadly shots rang. But to Naomi's surprise, behind the smoking barrel was the seven-year-old girl. Her arm extended as the driver fell to the ground, lifeless.

The light was green.

Naomi couldn't release the brake pedal, still she sat and watched. The father slowly stood up. The young girl hugged him, pistol still in hand. He pulled his smart phone out and gave it to his daughter. She smiled cheerfully accepting the phone, taking a picture of herself alongside the body.

It was bittersweet. Her first confirmed kill. A steppingstone to a better life and one of two ways to get pardoned from the Killzone.

Naomi smiled and pulled off. "Younger gets older every year."

CHAPTER 1

Naomi

Gentrification. I learned that word in one of my English classes right before graduation. They say that's what we're going through. When I say "they" I mean the media, blogs and everybody in between the sources. This supposed to be the reasons behind all the stores closing, people dying and things turning for the worst.

That wasn't the definition I was taught. I graduated with a 3.8 GPA. I learned that it meant the restoration of a deteriorated urban property, especially in the working-class neighborhoods. What I was witnessing was genocide, which meant systematic, planned annihilation of a racial, political, or cultural group.

They were killing us.

My name is Naomi, my friends call me Nay-Nay for short. I'm 19-years-old. In my short life thus far I've seen so much change. My innocence was long gone. I've been through too much.

It's always been rough in the city, but since the last terrorist attack in Washington, D.C. a few years back, it's tragic now. The government actually packed up and relocated to a undisclosed location. The once Chocolate City was now, The Killzone.

I live in Northwest, Washington. We call it uptown. The residents in other areas, including mines, don't call it "The District of Columbia" anymore. It's been dubbed, The District of Corruption.

After the atomic bomb was dropped in downtown D.C. destroying the White House, Capital and the monuments, just to name the most important. I guess the original plan was gentrification, but after a while we noticed they just wanted us out.

We wasn't going for that mess. Wouldn't any Black or foreign owners sell their homes, business or properties. That's when the government basically sectioned us off from the rest of the country by passing a bill that legalized a lot of laws that was once prohibited, but now legal only in the Nation's capital city. 'Sucks right?'

It's like I'm living in a 365-day purge, but this was not a movie and it wasn't for a few hours. There was no law enforcement except at borders making sure you don't try to leave out. Everyone owned a gun. The corner stores sold them like cigarettes. There aren't any hospitals for trauma victims, only for natural health problems. That's not even the worst part. People from all over the country can enter at their own risk and get paid to kill. That only placed us at the top of the target list.

The only way to leave The District was to tally up confirmed kills which are points. We can save money up too, as an alternate. The point system was bullshit. In short, absolute foolishness.

It basically helps the 'New Government' win. The population in the city was steadily dropping. I'm not even sure if it's still in the millions anymore. The meat wagon ride by faithfully, full.

You get 150 points for a confirmed black kill, 100 for any other race except white. You only get 10 points for white people.

"That's bullshit if I ever heard it."

If this wasn't genocide, I don't know what was. To leave the Killzone you needed 10,000 point or $150,000 cash, a person. I'm getting out of here no matter the cost or what I have to do, me and my little brother.

"Come on Khalil! Hurry up," I yelled through the house. "You know we have to hurry before it gets dark and crazy around there. They be thirsty around that neighborhood."

"Don't rush me witcho' scared ass. I got you if the boogieman try to take your cookies," I heard him snicker as I passed the bathroom door that he was behind.

"Whatever, punk! Come on." I balled my fist and banged the door one good time for good measure.

A simple task like going to the store to get food, drinks and toiletries could be detrimental. It had to be planned. I made my mind up that I wasn't going to get caught up like our parents did, underestimating the new world order.

They were both dead. I still remember the day it happened. I was 17-year-old and the government just declared the Killzone into legislation. The white people that voted against it and had money, quickly sold their homes next to nothing in price. The government offered them vouchers to return after the genocide, I mean gentrification. We didn't get the same vouchers. It's funny, only they received them options. To come back that is.

My parents purchased the house, thinking if we lived in this uppity ass Georgetown neighborhood, we would be safe until the tide turned. They were wrong. It was wishful thinking. The only thing it did was save me and my brother from the home invasion when me and Khalil ran to the panic room.

It was a Sunday and things were still normal for the most part, at least in my uptown neighborhood. A little boy that was on his paper route just placed the mail in the box. My father was in the driveway washing his car. He had a BMW 650 Coupe with a hard convertible top. This was something he did on a regular everyday weekend, even before we moved here.

I was on my phone texting my bestie, Diamond. I think Khalil was in the living room playing his game system. I was on the porch, so I could hear him cursing the television out. He loved that game. I forgot what me and Diamond were talking about. It was something about . . . wait, oh yeah. We was talking about our other friend Cortez. I call him Corty. I had a crush on him since forever, but he'll never know. Everyone else calls him Tez, but later for that.

My mother walked past, coming from inside the house and rubbed my head like a dog. I pushed her hand away and she giggled. She blew my daddy a kiss and walked down the driveway to retrieve the mail. I didn't think anything of it until I heard tires screech, then come to a halt.

I lifted my head from my phone and was shocked to paralysis. A caravan door slid open as she closed the mailbox. Two unmasked men jumped out with guns. I'll never forget their faces. The first gunman didn't waste any time as he shouted, "Money in da bank!"

My daddy tried to run to my mother, but when he made it to her all he could do was catch her lifeless body.

My little brother, Khalil came out of nowhere. I felt him grab me. My daddy yelled something to him, but I couldn't hear. My ears didn't work. My front door was slammed shut by Khalil and I did hear the last fatal shot ending my daddy's life. That was all she wrote.

It changed me forever.

I don't know if I passed out or what, but Khalil threw water on my face and I came to. He let me know the coast was clear. Coming out the panic room the house was flipped.

I dialed 911 and it was disconnected. No police. No help. No nothing. We had two options. Either call "Waste Management" to get our parents or bury them ourselves. We buried them.

CHAPTER 2

"Aye sis!" Khalil yelled down the stairs, grabbing my attention. "Did you see my vest?"

I felt the window to check the temperature. I didn't think it was cool outside.

"Vest?!" I frowned. "What vest?" But as soon as I said it I felt dumb and shook my head. "You talkin' 'bout your bulletproof one, right!"

"Naaahh! My Mr. Rogers vest, stupid."

I deserved that, but I'll never admit it to him, especially since I was wearing one.

"Look in the bedroom!" I told him after lifting my own shirt to check the straps on mines, making sure it's tight and secure.

It's been two and a half years since my parents were murdered. We kept the house, didn't really have any other options. My parents left us some money in the will, and we made the necessary adjustments to the house to make it safer. I wish I could have grown up in this neighborhood—well, at least back then when things were normal.

My mother would often talk about the improvements and additions that would someday be made on the house. As I looked around, in my opinion it didn't really need much. I did make some alterations just to keep her spirit in the house.

Khalil and I lived in an old brick house with three levels and a basement. You would have thought we was rich once upon a time, especially in this neighborhood. I stood in the living room on the ground level looking myself over. The mirror stood the length of the wall right beside the staircase. Khalil recalled himself painted last summer but didn't even prime the walls. His technique left the old cracks still visible.

I turned my body to the side to view my physique. I looked professional. I'm Black and Dominican. Standing five-foot four inches with light, caramel skin. I leaned closer to the mirror and noticed something in my eyes. It was sleep from my earlier nap. I began wiping it away, then arching my brows to compliment my round, hazel eyes. I looked around in search of my brush. My hair was wild and thick and naturally long. It stopped at the small of my back where it didn't curl. Recently I had it dyed, but I always change it. Usually, I just throw it in a ponytail and call it a day.

Khalil came down the steps. He was wearing what he always wore—blue, skinny jeans and a V-neck tee shirt. I don't know why I assumed he just might dress more casual, at least since he knew where we was headed. I had on my slacks and a short-sleeved blouse and my good loafers. When I seen what Khalil was wearing, I didn't like it that I was dressed up.

I looked in the mirror one more time as he passed me, and I shook my head.

'I'M NOT WEARING THIS SHIT.'

I thought Khalil read my thoughts when he said, "Where the hell you going looking like a secretary?" He tilted his head sideways. "I thought we were going to the church to get some free food 'n shit, not go to the service."

"Ah ha! Funny." I threw my brush at him and he caught it laughing. "Hold on, I'll be back." I ran up the stairwell two steps at a time.

The stairwell was narrow. On the wall headed up the stairs were family pictures leading to the top. My mother had them set up in an ascending trail with images from childhood up until now, well then. I'm two years older now.

Inside my room I started peeling off my clothes. I tossed them in the hamper and was left with my pink laced panties, a bra, a Teflon vest and an ankle holster on. Rummaging through my closet I grabbed a pair of joggers, a tee-shirt and a pair of Air Max's. I tossed each article of clothing on the bed before putting it on. My bed was spacious and soft. My daddy bought it on clearance. It was a California King Therapeutic Memory Foam Mattress. I loved it.

I checked the safety on my .380 and put it back on my ankle holster. I slid into my joggers. I had to slightly jump up and down to get my ass into them comfortably. I tightened the straps on my Teflon then finally pulled my shirt over my head. I was ready.

Taking two steps at a time, once again I was in the living room. I knew I didn't take that long, but I guess it was long enough for Khalil to jump on the beanbag couch and start playing some shooting game.

I walked behind him. "I'm ready, let's go! Do you have your protection, Stink?"

He blew a sigh. I knew he hated his nickname. "You damn right I do," he said, not even looking my way, but raising his shirt to reveal the Mac-11 with the 30 round 9mm clip setting on top of his polo briefs.

My brother Khalil, my little brother, is 16 years old, but going on 30. He swears that he is the big brother. he is taller than me standing at 5' 9. Females love him. I notice how they act around him. He is quiet around strangers. They think he is too serious. When in all actuality he just don't know them. All the little girls seem to surrender when he touch them. They whine and moan in his rapture. Some cry their pleasures through the walls. I've heard them say they love the way his teeth look in his mouth and how he wears his kicks.

Even some of my friends tell me they love the way he walks, like he's soon to own the world. That's my brother and I love him, but he still a asshole.

CHAPTER 3

Some people didn't believe the point system, or the grand total amount was possible or humane. Most people in my neighborhood have an unspoken truce to protect each other. But outside of our makeshift borders, you're on your own.

The city still provided the necessities like department stores, grocery stores, and things of that nature. Almost all the employees were residents of the surrounding areas and were exempt from execution. If you killed them, you would get no points. The only thing you would receive is a publicized bounty with immediate pardon from the Killzone as the reward. This went for actual killings inside of any establishments as well, but when you cross the threshold of any business, it's open season.

A few light taps upon the pane made me turn to the window. It was Diamond, my bestie since before this madness. She was crazy, not as insane, but consumed by enthusiasm and excitement. Since the District was renamed, she might be a little of the first crazy I mentioned at first.

Diamond was at the window with her arms wide, waving her hands frantically, but pointing to the door. I was thinking she was in some kind of trouble but dismissed the thought.

Usually if I head to town, we do it together anyway, but I talked to her earlier and she told me she had other plans, when she told me that I told Khalil to go with me. I waved her in, telling her to come in. The door was unlocked. I didn't understand why she knocked. She had the keys to my house just in case she was in need or being chased, or whatever. She basically lived here too, and a locked door wouldn't be the reason my friend don't make it.

She burst through the door as I looked in the mirror admiring my new change of clothes. It sounded more like a crash. "Bitch! You ain't gonna believe this shit!"

I turned around to her slamming the door shut and looking through the window with a face of dismay. Her energy put me back on alert. Khalil even paused his game and turned in our direction.

"What! What is it!?" My eyes were bubbled. I had genuine concern.

Her face softened, then turned into a smile. "I just saved a bunch of money on my car insurance by switch to—"

"Shut da fuck up!" I cut her off. "I thought something was really wrong witcho' ass." I rolled my eyes.

She tried to give me a hug. "Awww, come here. Did I scare the baby?" She wrapped her arms around me from the back, squeezing my arms tight to my side.

Khalil pressed the game back on and shook his head. Diamond seen it and smiled. "Hey stink! Did I have you worried too?" He didn't even acknowledge her. He just put his middle finger high in the air.

She giggled. "Is that how you really feel, boo!" She walked toward him; really, she skipped in a playful manner. Standing beside him as he sat, she asked, "Who are you talking to in that earpiece?"

Khalil put his index finger high in the sky then pointed to his crouch area with his arm still extended and said, "Deez nutz! Wanna talk to 'em?" and giggled.

Diamond didn't like that. She slapped him in the back of his head.

SLAP!!

Khalil cringed up. "Damn girl, you ain't have to hit me like that." He rubbed the back of his head and turned to face her. "A simple no, was fine."

"Shut up!" She turned on her heels headed back to where I was. "You still goin' shopping?" She stood in front of me, blocking the mirror.

"Yeah, but I hope you remember it was grocery shopping." I looked around her and called Khalil.

"Come on! How many times I have to tell you." He waved me off. "I'm not goin'. Cuban Zirconia right there, you don't need me."

Diamond wasn't going to let that go. She interjected. "It's Diamond, and it's flawless."

"Whateva, I ain't goin,' " he said, still playing the game.

I knew how to get what I want. All I had to do was pull at his heartstrings. I pouted and in a whiny voice said, "Daddy told you to look after me."

"Tsst, a'ight! Come on." He threw the controller on the floor and stood up.

'Works every time.'

The three of us left the house together. I pressed the button on my keychain, and it triggered my lockdown system to my house, courtesy of daddy's 'Will' money. This wasn't your average security system. That company 'BRINKS' didn't have anything on this machinery.

As soon as the pressure of my finger left the button, it initiated the locking sequence which slammed steel bars quickly to cover every windowpane, every doorway and it was complimented with electric currents flowing through each bar, thousands of volts. If you touch it, you good as dead. Wasn't any warning signs around my property. When you died from trying to enter, the body goes as a kill for me on the highest level. The cash and/or points goes to my account. A win, win.

We got in my car. I drove my daddy's BMW 650 Coupe. It was flashy and fast. I had it modified from its original features. I'm trying to save some more money so I could make it bulletproof. That is what everybody else was doing to their cars, plus it was cheap. Not for me, I'm still recovering from the security system. Bulletproofing was not in the cards right now. I did get it painted all black matte. I had black light covering and all black rims. At night I was a ghost.

Coming to a stop sign, I glanced over at Diamond. She looked like she didn't have a care in the world. After her little joke in the house, I didn't notice her outfit until now. "Girl, what are you wearing?"

She smiled. "You like?"

I looked back to the road and pulled off, not giving her an answer. Just shook my head.

She rolled her eyes. "Whatever, trick. Just because it's the apocalypse in the city don't mean I can't dress sexy and find me a man."

Khalil pushed the back of the headrest. "No need to look any further, Big Daddy right here." He spread his arms wide like he was presenting himself as a gift.

"Boy, you wouldn't know what to do with me witcho' young self. I need a man."

"Don't get no manlier than this," Khalil said, but through the mirror I saw him pointing to his crouch area, yet again.

'NASTY SELF.' I looked back to the road.

Diamond had on this one-piece bodysuit, but it didn't leave nothing to the imagination as I noticed her nipples protrude. Plus, it was white. We was headed to the church to get some free food, but she only came to try and catch a date. She did look good though, I can't lie. Diamond was short like me, light skin redbone with curves for days. I wish I had her thickness.

CHAPTER 4

Nothing was changed in the city, in the physical state of it. Only thing that was different was the young grew up and started to understand the city for what it was. The youth lived in such a complicated time of already defined alliances and shifting feuds that most didn't feel the energy or courage to change—just go with it.

Khalil didn't mind. He played the shooting game so much that he actually considered himself as 'THE HITMAN.' He didn't have a main circle of friends. The ones he did have lived on the other side of the city. He loved the new aged girls. Prostitution was legal and it wasn't no age restriction. I'm sure he had his share. I see him now in my mirror as I drive. He looking out the window at every girl we passed by.

There were so many good-looking young girls out there. Most of them had little to nothing on with crazy wigs acting like whoever their potential clients wanted them to be. They popped gum and rolled their uniform skirts higher to show their thighs. Back when I was in school only the "fast" girls did things like that to attract the boys. Now damn near everybody doing it. It was a cycle. I did it too.

Khalil. I know he loves it. I would see him on any given day look at them from the front porch as they walked on the other side of the street. He liked to watch them as the sun glistened off their skin. He especially likes their silk stockings and high heels. My brother was a creep! I guess all boys his age are. I giggled to myself and concentrated back on the road.

"Eyes up, ears open," I said as we passed the checkpoint leaving my neighborhood. I waved at my neighbor that dubbed as security in the daytime. He patted his F & N assault rifle and smiled with a head nod. I remember when he tried to sell me one of them. He and my daddy were friends. I know I would hate to be on the other side of them .223 shells.

My brother pushed the center console and it opened. I looked to see what he was grabbing. It was a silencer. "Where you get that from?" I asked. "That's a fat silencer."

"I got connects." He smirked, screwing it into his MAC=11 submachine gun. "And it's not a silencer. It's a suppressor, stupid." He smacked his teeth and shook his head like I was supposed to know all that.

The church that supplied the free food was downtown. It was still uptown, just down bottom. The neighborhood still rang bells after all these years. 9th Street Compound. The church sat in the middle of it on 8th Street. I had a boyfriend in that neighborhood once upon a time.

The church was named New Bethel Baptist Church. I was always leery coming through here. It felt like the dark ages. Most of the rowhomes were left vacant. Old police monitor trailers were still occupied and active, but with thugs, hustlers and gangsters, it was like they monitored their own hood.

Coming off Georgia Avenue I turned right on Florida Avenue riding past a CVS, then made a quick left on 8th Street. Riding down the street to my left was a school, and to my right was row-homes, the supposedly vacant ones.

"Duck!!!" Khalil yelled.

BOC! BOC! BOC! BOC! BOC!

I pulled over and pulled the makeshift bulletproof shed-like covering over my window. Diamond did the same, not knowing where or how many shooters it was. More shots came and ricocheted off the window.

I looked back to check on Khalil. His shed wasn't down. I noticed him pull a mask over his face. I reached over the seat, grabbing his arm. "You bad not!"

He snatched away. "Dad said protect you, right!" He pulled his gun out and got out of the car. He ran around the car and I lost the visual of him, but still heard the same type of shots attack the car. In that same second I heard a suppressed, muffled round go off, followed by multiples. Then silence. I slowly lifted my shed up and seen Khalil walking to a corpse.

"STINK!! GET BACK TO THE CAR!" I yelled.

He looked back and smiled. "I told you I'm the hitman and now it's time to collect."

Khalil went through the guy's pockets and grabbed his wallet and put it in his pocket. Then he laid beside the bloody body and snapped a selfie. I seen the flash.

The crazy part was after all that he stood up with that crazy looking mask that had big lips, big teeth and a tongue hanging and stood up reading a paper that came from the guy's pocket. I think he looked at me and shook his head. He picked the guy's gun up and jogged back to the car.

The guy was shooting some type of handgun that had a drum on it. Khalil got back in the car. Me and Diamond had the "What the fuck!?" expression. He looked up. "Somebody want you or us dead," he said bluntly, like it wasn't nothing.

I grabbed the paper, and it was a picture of my car. The reward was 75 grand. That's half of what you need to get pardoned. "Ain't this a bitch!" I said. Diamond's eyes got big after she snatched it and read it. "Damn bitch! Who did you piss off?"

"I don't know, but I'm gonna find out."
Diamond smirked.

CHAPTER 5

I pulled in the parking lot of the church. Surprisingly weren't any of my tires flat and my car was still running without any problems. The only default was the new holes on the door and side panel. That was one of my reasons for wanting to get the car bulletproof. When driving through different neighborhoods the youth was trigger happy and would shoot at vehicles passing by. The adults would too. But mainly children. In their young minds this was all they knew. Guns are made to kill, and kills grant you freedom. Sad.

My mind was everywhere. How was any sane soul suppose to ever get use to this? I just sat in the car for a second, trying to collect my thoughts. I seen Diamond staring at me, but I'm looking forward. She is cool, calm and collected. It was like she wasn't even in the car 10 minutes ago. "Is you ready or nah?" she asked after I never acknowledged her stare.

I blew a sigh. "Yeah, I guess." Khalil was looking around. His eyes attentive and calculated. "Hold on right quick," he said as he opened his door.

I was jittery. Just his movements had me looking in all directions frantically, even though on this property was a "safe zone." Khalil walked to the truck of the car. Through the rearview mirror I saw him look at me and point downward. He wanted me to unlock the trunk. I did. I wondered what he could want out of the trunk. The last time I opened it, there wasn't anything there but a spare tire and tool chest. I didn't even know he had that suppressor in the console beside me. Aware of that fact, it was no telling what he was going to retrieve.

This just put me on a higher alert. I needed to pay more attention to my little brother, especially in these times. The way that he was fearless and comfortable in the way that he just attacked our attacker, let's me know a lot. My little brother not so little anymore and my daddy's last words was etched in his heart. "TAKE CARE OF YOUR SISTER WITH YOUR LIFE."

I turned to Diamond. Her face was pressed against the window looking at every guy that pulled up and entered the church. "Aye hooka'?" I called out.

She looked over her shoulder to face me. "Hmm?"

"Nothing. I'm just tryna figure out who would put this contract out on us!"

"Us! Bitch, ain't nobody looking for no Ms. Diamond. That's your car in the pic." She whipped her hair.

I playfully pushed her shoulder. "Oh, is that right?"

She smiled. "You know I'm playing. But I don't have a clue to who would do this. I do know a guy that be accepting contracts and with a bounty like yours I'm sure he would have some info. I could ask him."

"Uhh duh. Ask him," I said, then looked directly into her eyes. "Make sure he don't come for me."

"I was gonna do that anyway."

I heard the trunk slam and Khalil came around to the driver's side where I was seated and opened my door. I looked at him but didn't move. He was officially tripping. He was trying to give me this big automatic shotgun. Later I found out it was a AA-12. "Churches are safe zones." I pushed the gun away. "Can't nobody do shit on the property. That includes the parking lot. This ain't no department store or no shit like that when only the store is safe."

He didn't move. He squatted on a knee to be eye level with me. "Sis, do you think people really care about the rules?" Concern could be felt through his words.

"Yes!" I said matter-of-factly. "If they don't want a bounty on their head."

He pointed to the flyer that laid in the center console and shook his head. "A bounty didn't make you run home after they just tried to flip this joint. Ain't restrictions to a gangster with a gun and a under the table bounty on your head. Even Jesus' house ain't gonna stop a nigga from collectin' on dat' doe cheese."

I sat and pondered on everything he just said. I didn't want to admit it to myself, but he was right. He made a lot of sense. At the same time, I wasn't walking into no church with that big shotgun visible in my hand. He stared into me, waiting for a response. This was crazy, but normal in the new world—well, city of Washington. I inhaled a big breath. I couldn't accept it. "Give me something else. That shit too big. I'm not walking around with that."

"Tsst here." He smacked his teeth. I knew I was starting to irritate him. I didn't care. He lifted his shirt and pulled out the MAC-11 like that was a difference. I looked at him like he was crazy. That game he always playing must have had his mind gone or he really thought this was okay. Maybe it was me. It's hard to accept the new reality of things.

"You know what," I stood up out of the seat and he backed up a few steps. "You keep that. I got this." I reached for my ankle holster and pulled out my .380, putting it on my hip. "Happy?" I smiled, posing.

Diamond interjected. She climbed over my seat and stood beside me reaching. "Shid you trippin'. I'll take that." She grabbed the submachine gun. "After that shit we just went through, I'll bust them deacons in there if they look crazy." She reached back into the opening of the glove compartment. Khalil smiled at the view and smacked her ass. "Boy, stop!" she said, turning around with a mean mug and a mean arch in her back. She grabbed a shoestring and tied it around the gun and put it on her shoulder like a purse. She put her hand on her hip. "You like the new Gucci?"

I ignored her comment. I tried to look to see what else was in the glove compartment. It seemed like everybody knew what was in my car but me. Diamond got out of the car and Khalil cautiously kept watch. One of the deacons came out of the church and held the door open. We made it to the door. He shook his head in a disapproving manner. I understood where he was coming from without any words yet to be exchanged. "It's sad that you all have to bring that type of artillery in the Lord's house," he said.

I wanted to but didn't respond. I passed him offering him a greeting. Khalil didn't mind expressing himself. "Yeah, I hear you preacher man, but I'd rather not be on the other end of one of your eulogies, so I came prepared."

Diamond smiled as Khalil passed the deacon. "Hey preacher man, you like my new Gucci?" She laughed at her own joke and the deacon just shook his head.

There was a line in the sanctuary. It reminded me of a soup kitchen line. We stood in the back; it inched closer and closer. The church was in great shape. It had the colorful windows, the expensive kind that had all types of spiritual signs and symbols.

The pews were clean with bibles behind each bench with fans. As the food was being given out, the Pastor was offering a sermon. Most of the older people that already received their food, found a seat to listen. Every time he would stop to take a breath, I would hear an iPod or someone's phone loud through the earbuds.

I followed the sound and my eyes landed on my boo. He wasn't my "boo" officially, just my other best friend. Cortez. He was in line bobbing his head, waiting to get his food. My heart started to pound. It did this every time I seen him. "He's so HAND-SOME," I thought. He knew it as well, with his conceited self. That's why I never approached him. I wasn't going to be a part of his flock. We already friends and partners in crime. All three of us earn money together; the motivation being an exit plan. I've noticed my brother been trying to get more involved. I've heard rumors.

The music in Cortez's ear had his shoulders jumping as he rapped the words. He could have been in the video how serious he looked. I smiled to myself. I walked over to him, but on a slow creep trying to spook him. I was right on him. I grabbed his shoulder. That was a bad idea. Before I could say the line, I re-hearsed in my head, in a swift quick motion he grabbed my arm, spun me around into a headlock and had a Glock 40 touching my temple.

"Oh my God, Corty it's me!" I was scared. He sniffed my hair.

"Nay-Nay! Is this you?" He asked a stupid question. He knew exactly who I was.

"Yeah boy, let me go!!"

"Damn, you smell good." He loosened his grip from my neck, but kept one arm slightly around my neck, his other arm slowly dropping, feeling me up, landing on my waistline where he pulled me close. I can't lie. It felt so good. "You know you can't be running up on me like that baby girl." He rubbed my thighs, stopping right at the v of my crouch where I stopped him.

"Get off me, freak!" I playfully snatched away, even though I loved being in his embrace. I wanted to salvage the feeling.

Khalil and Diamond walked up and stood where we was. We all basically cut the line. Nowadays people let so much go, especially when it was a group of young youth.

Cortez spread his arms wide to greet Khalil. My brother and Cortez were cool too. They were like brothers and Khalil loved when he was around. I be thinking that Cortez was a big reason why Khalil as getting more violent.

"Wat' up, lil bro!" Cortez spoke. "I see ya came to get your free shit too!"

Diamond popped him on his head. "WATCH YOUR MOUTH! We is in a church."

"Maaaann, FUCK church! You act like you don't see the life we livin.' Look at you. You got a choppa purse." He pointed to her MAC-11 hanging on her side. "Talking 'bout watch my mouth, girl if you don't get da' fuck."

I just shook my head as the line moved forward. Cortez could be a bit much. He is so blunt all the time, no filter. He seemed to always have one hell of a day. He turned to face all of us and began one of his stories. I call them adventures. I just listened.

"Y'all ain't gonna believe this shit." We all gave each other a knowing look. "No bullshit! Why I was driving right, and this gangsta ass squirrel jumped in front of my car. I swerved to try to avoid him right, but the lil' nigga acted like he wanted beef." He took a step back and got real animated. "He stood on two feet and it looked like he was muggin '. . .'"

"Stop it! Go ahead wit dat bullshit, homes," Khalil said, laughing.

"Nah for real. He was muggin' so I swerved that bitch right in his direction. You know what I did. Yup I ran his ass over. The crazy part is it's almost like he wanted me to run him over. When I got close, I saw him do the cross your heart, hope to die and looked to the sky." He imitated.

Diamond was cracking up. "Shut up, boy! Was you high?"

Cortez looked to the sky. "A little . . . I think." He started to scratch his head. "Man, I don't know. But what I do know is that new shit I had, like dat!!"

I love that boy. That was his only default in my eyes. He loved to get high. In these times I understood that people like to chase a getaway. Anywhere better than this. He be fine when he smokes weed, but when he smokes that P.C.P. or that deuce (K2) he be lunch' (tripping) good. Like at that moment, he really believes the squirrel committed suicide. I stood there wondering if he thought he could get points for that kill.

We made it to the front and grabbed our bags. I'm the only one that thanked the elderly ladies that gave us our groceries. Everybody else just grabbed the food and kept it pushing.

Leading the way was Cortez. He had his arm around Khalil's neck, leaning over and whispering in his ear as they walked. I couldn't hear what they were saying as I tried to catch up and do a little eavesdropping on the conversation. All I could make out was, "It's gonna be easy," before Diamond's voice over powered.

"Slow down, nosey." She was right on my heels. She knew me well. Without exchanging words, she already knew what I was doing, but she didn't care. She had her own prerogative. "So, what we bouta' do since it ain't nobody in here for me?"

"You a hoe," I joked with her. "That's all you be thinking about."

Standing in the parking lot I noticed it was still a couple hours of daylight in the sky. That was a good thing. At night it could get real hectic, especially in this neighborhood. Actually, it was my old neighborhood that I grew up in before my parents decided to move me and Khalil to the Georgetown neighborhood.

The shooting came back to mind as I looked up the street where thirty minutes ago somebody tried to cash in on me. It couldn't be a coincidence that the first attack I encountered was around here. The enemy list could be long, or very short. Thinking some more the hit could be on me or my brother. All that was advertised was my car. I needed to get more information. All cellphone activity was monitored and contracts like this one had to be on the dark web.

I didn't really want to go to the library; at least not by myself. Last time I did that I seen a guy walk straight into one of the cubicles and blow a dude's head off his neck. The worst part was the reason why. The victim checked out the last copy of a book after he cut the line. Crazy. Shit gets real. It could get set off any given moment.

"Excuse me Ms.!!" I heard a voice from the sidewalk. "Do you have a minute?" he asked. I was messing with Diamond about her hoeish ways when I heard it. I turned to the voice and he was waving me over. Let Diamond tell it, he was calling for her, but I knew better.

"Move, bitch," she whispered only so I could hear. "He talking to me." Diamond slightly, but aggressively pushed me, stepping in front of me. She just knew she had one as her all-white skin-tight bodysuit hugged her curves. She was stacked, but I knew he wanted me.

I couldn't help but chuckle at her walk. She was confident. The guy waved her off and pointed to me. The guy was cute too. He stood like he was a shy schoolboy who had a crush on a girl and finally built up enough confidence to call her. He was twisting one foot like he was playing with something under his foot with both arms behind his back. His demeanor put a natural smile on my face.

Cortez's face was contorted as I approached the guy. I thought it was cute that he appeared jealous. I made sure I put a little extra on my walk so he could see what he was missing out on. I looked back to try and catch him staring, but it's like he ignored me. He turned the other way and started speed walking to the 8th Street sidewalk exit as I walked toward S Street.

I was in my feelings a little bit. That just made me move more willingly to see what was up with this chocolate man. I looked back to see Diamond with her hand on her hips. I smiled at her. Khalil was stacking the trunk with the food we just received.

I stopped a few feet in front of the guy. Maybe three. He was a rugged cute. I could tell he was from the hood, a thug. 'JUST MY TYPE.' My smile was natural. "Hey."

It was weird. He looked at my feet. I think then back to my eyes and then smiled. It got a little weirder when he asked me to come closer. I was only a couple feet away and could hear him just fine. To my right I noticed a presence approach in my periph-eral. It was Cortez walking like he was an alien or something. The guy was so into me he didn't notice. I didn't pay it no mind. 'I KNOW HE WANT ME.' I thought about Cortez as he neared. I decided to rub it in. "Come here, boo," the guy said, bringing my attention back to him. I embraced it and took two steps forward and his hand dropped from behind his back, then raised his arm; a pistol in his hand.

"Shit!" I froze.

"Sorry Ms. Lady, but I gotta get outta this city." I closed my eyes.

BOC! BOC! BOC!

I felt blood splatter on my cheek. It was warm and thick. I opened my eyes as I wiped the DNA off my face. I saw Cortez running up, gun in hand. He stopped in front of a twitching corpse and fired a few more shots. "Night, night fool." He kicked the body a couple times. "Nigga you tried to kill my boo." I smiled when he called me that. "Not today, nigga!" he said looking at the body.

I jumped in his arms and hugged him. "Oh my God, thank you so much Corty! You saved my life."

"Yeah, I kind of did. I knew something was up with Slim. I seen him when I pulled up." He released me from the hug. "You know I been around here. I was in the store when I heard some shots—"

I cut him off. "Yeah, that was for me. Some dude fired shots at the car before we made it here. Khalil got out like he was crazy and killed the shooter."

"Oh yeah! But inside the store I seen this fool reading this." He bent over and went in the guy's pocket, pulling out the same bounty I already had. "I thought it was your car, but really didn't give it a second thought. That was until I seen him again calling you over. You know you can't kill on the property. Some people respect that law, and he was one of them. He was tryna get you to come to the sidewalk as you so sweetly did."

I shook my head in disbelief at how stupid I was. I was trying to make him jealous, but he was on point and gave me another chance at life. Khalil and Diamond ran to my side. "You okay, girl?" Diamond asked.

I was lost for words. All I wanted to do was get out of there. I looked at Cortez again. He was kneeled over the guy, going through his pockets. He was getting proof of the kill, then he did the same thing Khalil did. He took a selfie.

CHAPTER 6

Two Weeks Later

It's been a couple weeks since I been through my old neighborhood. I'ma be honest, I've been a little weary about the shootout. It kind of slowed my motivation down in my pursuit of money. Really, I was waiting to hear back from Diamond. She told me that today would be the day I'll get some type of information. Hopefully, this was true. I didn't like being cooped up on the house.

Today I felt a little better than yesterday. Hopeful. That would be a good feeling to describe it. Before my mother died, she started a vegetable garden. It was her little slice of heaven. She always wanted to limit the reasons for leaving, so it was pretty big. My favorite section in the garden was the tomato section. it was the post peaceful, at least how I had it set up around a bunch of rose bushes.

In the garden and when I'm by myself I always try to extend my talent in yoga. I sat Indian style, sipping my tea and tried to extend my leg upward. When my leg was extended upward, I placed the cup of tea in the center of my extended foot. It wasn't easy, but I completed it.

I stayed in the garden for a while. Thoughts of what I planned on doing to my assailant flooded my mind. Whoever it was had it coming, but not before I understand the why. To get a straight up answer I knew I was going to give off the illusion that I was to let them live. After I get all the information I needed, then will I grant the same fate that they wished on me.

I still wasn't sure what the gender of the person was. Really it didn't matter. I truly couldn't think of anyone that I could have pissed off to this extreme. Nobody I knew had that much money to cover that kind of payout. Seventy-five grand. Just to throw away on measly ol' me. Yeah, I need answers.

The meditation I just completed was rejuvenating. I really need it. Looking at my watch I noticed I was out here for three hours. I stood up and enjoyed a nice stretch. A few bones cracked, but in the right places. I grabbed the water pail and watered each section of the garden starting with the tomatoes.

Entering the house, the temperature was a little humid. I opened the fridge and grabbed a bottle of smart water. I drank most of the bottle and put the remaining content back. I climbed the stairs. Each step I took I dropped an article of clothing. First, was my headband, wristband and towel. My hair fell past my shoulders after I released my ponytail. Next, was my dry fit tank top. I didn't wear a bra. My small, but perky breast stood straight and round, no sag. The cool air from the air conditioning stiffened my gumdrop nipples. I didn't really like the size of my chest. In a separate saving stash was money that I planned to get my boob job.

There were plenty of surgeons that got stuck in the city and would do procedures for cheap, compared to the original prices, just so they could get out.

The next layer was my yoga pants. They were thin and comfortable. I entered my room and came out of those too and kicked them to a corner. That left me with a pair of boy short panties on. I pulled my wedgy out and jumped on my bed and sunk into my extra soft comforter.

Grabbing the remote I turned on the TV. The first thing that appeared on the screen was the news. It was the only local channel. The news wasn't the same anymore. There wasn't a meteorologist, anchorman or none of the elements of a broadcast station. There was one guy reading the death toll for the day, unnamed, or claimed bodies. New contracts and bounties of those that broke the law was pictured and exposed.

Regular TV was non-existent. All you could watch was Internet TV. Networks like Netflix, Hulu and things of that nature was available. I loaded my Netflix account and stopped on a favorite, BOONDOCKS. It was in my recent watch. It had the complete first three seasons. I loved that show. It always had my eyes wet and cramps in my ribs from laughter. I pressed PLAY ALL and the first episode began.

I got through about two shows before my phone rang. It was Cortez. "What you want, boy?" People knew I didn't like to be interrupted when I'm watching my show. This was my soap, Oprah.

"Other than you," he paused. It made me smile. I'm glad he couldn't see me blush.

"In your dreams, Corty. Now stop playin.' I'm watching my show. What you want?"

"That's crazy how you do me but listen. I need you. Are you down for this move? Before you answer, you goin.' Your ass need to get out the house. I need my girl Nay-Nay back. I'm tired of Naomi."

I blew a sigh. I was conflicted. "I dunno, maybe. It depends on when. I'm not tryna really leave until I find out who put this hit on me."

"Fuck dat! Ain't nobody gonna do shit to you. Big daddy got you."

"Boy bye," I told him after I laughed in his ear. I heard Diamond coming up the stairs. She was singing loud. I leaned to try to see down the hallway. "You funny, you know that. But—"

"Fuck that shit you talkin.' I'm on da way." Click.

"Hello . . . hello!? I know dis nigga didn't hang up on me." I tossed the phone on the bed and laid back.

A few seconds later Diamond came through the door, loud as always. "Hey girl!" she spoke. I gave her a half wave as I put some hot Cheetos in my mouth. "Why you got your titties all out? And them little ass panties. It looks like your lips 'bout to burst through them. Ugh, why you ain't shave" she said, going through my dresser and tossing me a sports bra and some little shorts.

I didn't understand what the problem was. She knew how I do when I'm home alone. Khalil left out early this morning to do what God only knows. As long as he was safe and protected, I was cool. "Don't come in here messin' wit me," I said, pulling the bra over my head. "Did you find out anything about the guy yet? It's been two weeks.," I said, getting a little impatient.

"Actually, I did. He wants us to meet him tomorrow. I think he wants some money or something. He didn't say it, but it was implied."

"Is that right? We'll see what he talking 'bout." I turned my attention from her back to my show and pressed PLAY. I had it paused since Cortez called.

Everybody was trying to get in the way of my show. It was crazy. They all knew how I felt. I didn't play when it came to THE BOONDOCKS. Riley was my favorite character, next in line was granddad. Riley reminded me of Khalil when he was young, bad as shit. Granddad was just too funny, period.

Diamond stood staring at me. I guess she had more to say, but I wasn't going to ask. She sat on the bed with me, then snatched my bag of Cheetos. I smiled. I knew she was in her feelings about how I kind of brushed her off.

It wasn't intentional. I just needed answers. My damn life was on the line. Everyday a new person visits the dark web and reads the ad, and the target grows on my back. She had to understand that.

After a couple more episodes and some girl talk, the screen on my TV turned blue. In that same second it came back on with a picture of my front yard and driveway. The wall behind me exposed my stash as it raised up like a storefront, revealing my arsenal of weapons.

The new security system I had installed included this with the premium package. Pulling in the driveway was Cortez. His music was loud, his car was louder, and I wasn't talking about the pipes. It had a louder presence. He had an old 1996 Chevy Caprice painted orange with the Dunkin Donuts logo and sprinkles all over it. He had a lift kit with 26-inch rims. LOUD.

Diamond jumped up. "Bitch! What is all this?" I smiled as I put the code in, and the wall came back down, and the show continued.

"You know I'm not playing. If somebody think they pulling up on me, they got another thing coming."

I got up and put some jeans on and another shirt. I didn't want Cortez getting any sneak peeks. I went to the bathroom to freshen' up. I still couldn't understand why Cortez had that effect on me. Diamond laughed at me. She knew what I was doing and why. I didn't care.

"Get out! Go let him in and get out my face." I closed the door after pushing her out.

I heard her go down the steps. I paused my show and turned to the channel where my CV camera was on so I could watch. I had to pay extra for audio.

Cortez got out the car. Diamond came into view after closing the door, standing on the porch. I seen Khalil get out the passenger seat. It surprised me. That put a curious feeling inside me as I leaned closer to the monitor.

"Where y'all coming from?" Diamond asked. I ate Cheetos like I was watching a movie.

"Chillin,' killin' and getting laid," Khalil said all too smoothly. I shook my head as I watched. Cortez grabbed Khalil and turned him to face him. "Don't tell your sister I had you with me doin' nothin. She'll kill me."

"YOU DAMN RIGHT!" I said to myself, looking at the screen like he could hear me.

"What y'all 'bout to do now?" Diamond asked as they neared.

"I'm 'bout to get Naomi big head ass out this house so she can relieve some stress. Big Dawg style."

"Boy, she ain't goin' like that!" Diamond frowned. It was funny.

THAT'S RIGHT BOO! TELL HIS ASS.

"Shut up! Ain't nobody talking 'bout like that. I got a move for all of us."

That was all I heard before they entered the house. I turned the camera off and jumped back in the bed. I pressed PLAY and skipped an episode in case Diamond tried to be funny and put me on blast.

They all came in my room talking like I wasn't even in the room. Cortez jumped on my bed laying right beside me. Khalil sat at the foot and Diamond went straight to the mirror. She stayed in the mirror. They all kept talking for about three minutes and still didn't acknowledge me.

"Uh, excuse me!" I said. They all looked at me. "I'm doin' fine, thanks for asking. What about y'all?"

It was quiet for a second. Everybody looked at me staring like I was crazy, then in unison they continued talking.

WOW, I thought.

I rolled off the bed. It's that big. California King. I was about to leave the room. "Aye Nay-Nay!" Cortez called me, stopping me in my tracks. I turned to face him. "I hope you ready. We 'bout to go on this move and hit this store. You down, right?"

"Hit a store? You can't do that, you know that," I said. "We ain't 'bout to go kill in there."

"Doh. We ain't gonna kill nobody, just relieve some aggression and get paid while doin' it," he said.

I thought about it. Really, I didn't mind. I did need to get out the house and get back on my shit. I do need money if I'm trying to get up out of here. "Fuck it, let's go."

CHAPTER 7

I was in the blind. I didn't even know the full extent of the move. All I knew is it was go time. This was the first time I ever had my little brother with me on a move. I've never seen him work and he never witnessed my work either.

I put all the necessary locks and codes on my house to secure safety. Cortez wanted to drive his car. I declined and told him to pull the car in my driveway and into the garage. My car was in the shop getting body work.

We had to ride in Diamond's car. She owned a Cadillac Deville. You couldn't tell her that she wasn't the shit. Even though she stole it from a precious move we did, she treated it like it was her own. She had it pained candy red and it smelled like the blunt blast spray. There was a blunt in the center console when I sat in the passenger seat. I grabbed it and sparked it.

"Damn Hefa!" Diamond was a little mad. I didn't care, I needed this. "You just gonna spark my shit?"

"Yeah and . . ." I rolled my eyes and inhaled the potent intoxicant.

She shook her head and started the car. We pulled off. The ride cool and smooth. The only thing that threw me for a loop was that she listened to all R&B tracks. I couldn't really get in the mood for what we were about to do, and she wouldn't change it.

Luckily, I had my phone and earbuds. I listened to some old 3 6 Mafia and I was ready. We pulled in front of the store. I got out the car first. I was grateful to have an easy job today. I still wasn't comfortable with Khalil here, but it was already in progress.

Inside the store was wide and spacious. It had a variety of products from your everyday corner store stuff to the type of things you get from Walmart. It was a one-stop shop. I'm surprised I never shopped here before. I was impressed.

I was a little hungry, so I decided to set up my recon spot in the foot court. I could see the whole store and side entry and exit ways. I ordered some chili cheese fries and began to eat. The cheese and chili was torch. My face was in the container when I heard, "Bitch! Stop playing wit' me and put the money in da' bag!" It was Khalil.

I never seen him in that light before. "Fuck dem tears! That shit ain't gonna stop me from doing what da' fuck I have to do!" He moved closer. "Bitch, I swear to God if you even think about trying to alert somebody, I'll decorate that chip rack with a new flavor of you."

The lady was so scared that I felt sorry for her. But on the other hand, this the city we live in and she know that. She sniffed the snot from her nose. "O . . . Okay, please don't kill me. I have a child at home," the female store clerk said.

Cortez decided he wanted some of the fun. He wanted to play the empathetic robber. "Listen lady, my friend over here don't give a fuck about your seed, but I do. I have kids myself."

LIES! I thought as I listened.

"But the longer you take the longer this day gonna be, and I mean for us cause he gonna kill you."

Khalil stepped back in front of Cortez. "Fuck dis!" He raised his fully loaded 45 Smith and Wesson to her head, then lowered it to her shoulder.

BOOM!

She flew back and fell on the floor. Her apron oozed blood as it got heavy around her neck. A guy came bursting through one of the side doors and was about to run right past me. He had a gun in hand. I pushed a chair in his path. He fell over, dropping the gun he had. I stood up and was right on top of him.

"Stay down!" was my only words.

Cortez jumped over the counter. "Aye Kali, you wild boy," he said as he looked over at the tobacco products. "Bag all this shit up, lil bruh." Cortez was having a hard time opening the register. It wasn't such an easy task. He, nor any of us ever used one before.

BEEP! BEEP! BEEP!

"Man, what the fuck?! This joint dumb ass shit," he said pressing damn near every button. He started to get frustrated. I could see it all in his face. "Fuck this shit!" he maxed.

BOC! BOC! BOC!

He shot the register and it popped open like a jack-in-a-box. "Ain't this bouta' bitch!" He looked mad. I don't know how much money was in there, but I could tell he wasn't satisfied. "Watch her!" Cortez told Khalil. "Bring him over here, boo," he told me.

I made the guy get up and we walked toward Cortez. "Sit cho' ass down, nigga!" he told the store owner. The owner cut and crawled to be closer to the woman. It was my guess that it was his wife. "Come wit me," Cortez told me.

We walked to the back of the store and found the security footage. The store was ancient. They still had VHS. I ejected the tape. I looked around some more and spotted a nice size safe door ajar.

"I know it ain't this easy," I said, grabbing Cortez' attention.

We both walked over to it. He smiled. "What do we have here?"

I guess we came in at the right time. It looked like they were about to deposit cash this morning. The money was in neat stacks, but in bank plastic slips. I followed Cortez' eyes and he spots a trash can. He emptied its contents. He filled it up with the money we just found.

This lick kind of made my day. We were about to exit the store when Cortez stopped again. This time he grabbed three "fif's" of Remy and two bags of rap snacks.

"WOW!" I shook my head.

CHAPTER 8

Diamond drove through the city like the law was behind us. She ran lights and merged lanes without warning. A couple of times she almost hit pedestrians crossing inside the crosswalk. Sitting in the passenger seat, I sat watching the streets fly by.

In the back Khalil and Cortez talked amongst themselves. I couldn't really hear their conversation between tires screeching and whatever was playing through the speakers. Diamond had a weird taste in music. Maybe she was just a lot more open to different genres than I was.

Watching her drive, my head naturally shook. She had her arms wrapped around the steering wheel as if she was taking a nap and the seat was extra close. God forbid if we crash. She was headed straight through the windshield. Let her tell it, she was the best driver in our clique. I smiled at the thought.

Khalil was seated behind Diamond. As I looked at him, the respect I had for him grew. It wasn't that I didn't respect him. It was just that in my eyes he was still my "little" brother. Seeing him now, I started noticing more of daddy's attributes bursting through. That was a good thing, but today clearly shows he still reckless and still have room to grow.

"Stink!" I yelled over the music. He looked at me with an irritated mug. I didn't care if he didn't like his nickname. He ain't care when he was younger, and our parents called him that. He done got a little bass in his voice and hair on his nuts. He think he grown. I gave him the same look in return. "What you did today was stupid and reckless. What if that lady was to die? Your ass would be the new face on the broadcast, then what?!" I scolded him.

"I wouldn't have gotten caught. We got the tape duh! And I had on deez." He raised his hand, showing me the gloves, he had on. "Thank goodness for these good ol' OJ's." He took one off and dangled it. "If it don't fit, you must acquit."

Everybody in the car laughed. I didn't find it funny. He wasn't no damn O.J. Simpson and he for damn sure didn't have the dream team. He didn't understand my frustration or the seriousness of this. Every time it's an unclaimed murder or death in a restricted area, there was a full-blown investigation. The investigators that are brought in specialize in their craft. They had a ninety-five percent success rate. So, them measly gloves he was dangling wasn't nothing. I needed him to understand that.

Making it back to the house Diamond skidded to a stop. She was driving so reckless that she almost drove into my garage. Inside the house we all sat on the couch in the living room. Cortez kneeled on the middle of the floor after sliding the dining room table out of the way.

Emptying the trash bag that was full, all the contents dropped out everywhere. There was twenty cartons of Newport's, twelve boxes of backwoods, ten thousand dollars in cash, three fif's of Remy and two bags of Rap snacks. Khalil's eyes went straight toward the chips. Cortez noticed him looking. "Uh uh nigga. Ain't no need you lookin' at my chips . . . No greedies!" he said, grabbing the bags and licking his tongue. Khalil looked sad as Cortez sat beside me putting his arms around my shoulder, teasing him. I snatched a bag and opened them. He looked like he wanted to protest. The expression on my face made him think otherwise.

He shrugged his shoulders. "That's fine. I guess no greedies don't hold weight 'round here no more," he said as I took a couple, then gave the rest to Khalil. "Then you gonna pass the bag around too." He slapped a pack of Newport's on the palm of his hand before opening them, shaking his head. "You ain't even gotta act like that." I waved him off.

Khalil and Diamond started counting the money for reassurance. They put it in four piles of twenty-five hundred a piece. That was the payout for the caper. Cortez stood up and grabbed his stack. He noticed that nobody touched the tobacco products.

"Oh, y'all too good for jacks in shit, huh? Don't trip." He began placing them back into the bag. "I'ma take 'em around da way and sale em. Just like I do anything else."

"Leave me a couple cartons," Diamond said. "I'ma give it to my mother when she come back." I shook my head sadly.

Diamond still held onto the thought that her mother was coming back. It's been almost three years and she was yet to return. No mail, no money, no nothing. Just empty promises to return with more funds to get her out. I remember it like it was yesterday. Her mother ran off with a guy from work. He had money and lots of it, but not enough for the "both" of them. I understand she loved her mother, but in these times, you just don't leave your child to fend for herself.

Cortez gave her a few cartons then stood up and slung the bag like a satchel. "A'ight peeps, I'm outta here! I'll catch you on da rebound."

Khalil was thumbing through his money but looked up after hearing Cortez. "Where you bouta go?"

"Round da way to make some mo' money!" he bragged.

I hated when he did stuff like that around Khalil. It was exciting to him, by enticing him obviously to want to do it. Cortez didn't seem to understand the influence he had over Khalil. He was the big brother he never had.

The last thing I wanted Khalil to do was start hustling. That would leave him vulnerable for anyone to come through and get an easily confirmed kill and payout. Couldn't tell him that he "Mr. Hitman."

I remember when all this started. The whole genocide. As a clique we decided we had to do something. But before that, me, Diamond, and Cortez were called the terrible three. Best friends since early childhood. I'm talking early as diapers. Our parents were close. They grew up on the same block too. The only difference is we went to the same daycare, elementary, junior high and high school.

Cortez stopped going to high school right before the bill was signed. As soon as the bill was announced, Cortez gave me my first gun. In his backyard I was taught how to shoot. Learning quick, my skill set superseded his. Originally, it was just for protection. As the time passed, we needed the skills for money too. "We needed to get the hell out of here."

The plan was to start hustling and save to pay our fare. I didn't have no money, neither did Diamond. Cortez had just got a little money from his parents' accident. That's when he got all that mess done to his car and brought a lot of guns. With the remaining cash he purchased two pounds of weed. After about two weeks he didn't turn a profit. He smoked most of it with me and other friends around the way. We didn't make no money.

Realizing that hustling as a group wasn't our ticket or claim to fame, we figured the guns would serve a better purpose. Cortez continued to sell drugs too. He stayed around the way. It wasn't a fact, but I think he did. I never seen him make a transaction or he never mentioned it to me, but I'm not blind. The way he be on the phone and jump up to leave randomly, was all movements of a hustler.

"I'm 'bout to go with you," Khalil said.

"No, you ain't!!" I stood up. "I need your help in the house today. You've been gone all day."

He frowned. "Help doing what?!"

"Help doing whatever the hell I need you to do," I said walking to the door, opening it for Cortez. He looked at Khalil. "Listen to da warden, lil' bro. I'll come back on visiting hours." He smiled.

I pushed him out the door. "Bye, boy!!" and slammed it shut before he could say anything. Diamond was giggling. She always seem to think everything was hilarious. I looked at her. "Ain't nothing funny."

She smiled and raised her hand in surrender. "I'm sorry Warden. Please don't lock me down too." She walked backwards, up the stairs with her hands still up.

Smart ass.

I looked to see Khalil staring at me. "So, what you need help doing?" he asked.

"Nothing. You just ain't going right back outside after what we just did. Chill," I said walking off and leaving him with an irritated expression.

I'm Da Warden! I climbed the stairs.

Winded. That would the best way to describe the feeling after making it to the third level. Diamonds' area. It seemed like we all had our own floor. I opened her room door to see her on her stomach with her legs up, bent at the knees wiggling her toes. In front of her was a laptop with a guy on the screen.

She didn't hear me come in. It was dark with a low light setting. I was shocked to what my ears heard through the computer speakers in a low, but demanding tone, "You like dis' bitch! You think you could handle it?"

I slowly crept closer to get a closer look at the screen. WOW, I thought looking at the girth of the man as he stroked himself. Diamond let off a moan. "Yeah daddy, I can handle all that!" she seductively licked her lips.

"Bitch!" She turned to my voice.

"What the hell your freak ass in here doing?"

I know I scared her. She slammed the computer shut quickly before admitting. "Damn, girl! You scared the shit out me. I was making some money, but you fucked that up," she said, sitting up to face me. "You would be surprised what these guys pay for nowadays."

"You trickin,' bitch!"

"Hell no! But we could," she said in a lowered tone. "You could tease, fuck, get fucked or oral either way you like it." She shrugged. "Really, whatever you into and they pay good. Most of them rich!"

This was new information to me. The more I thought about it, the more it made sense. Tricking, prostitution or whatever you want to call it is legal. You set your own prices. I definitely didn't know about the site that was up. Diamond showed me her profile. Her pictures were cute. I liked her profile picture. She was showing off. After the tour of the site, I had to know.

"How long you been on the site? You know, active?"

"Just started. The guy that you seen was only my second john. He sent me a request for some virtual love and that's easy."

"You ever do it in person?"

"Nope! Not yet, but I've been thinking about it."

"Hmmm, open the site back up, sign me up."

Chapter 9

"Ouch!!" I yelled waking up. "What the hell was that for?" I asked Khalil. I threw the oversized pillow back at him. "Get up! You got that loud ass alarm clock. It wakes everybody up except you," he said walking away in boxers with a sleepy face.

I rolled over and looked at my digital clock. "Shit!" I jumped out of bed. I was about to be late. Was supposed to be headed around my way to pick up some more ammo and electric wiring for our property. I met the guy online. He agreed to meet me in a neutral place, which led me to choosing my neighborhood. I wasn't safe and neither was he, so we were even in his eyes.

A quick shower was all I needed to wake up. After calling and confirming our meeting, putting clothes on, I called for Diamond. She didn't answer so I called for Khalil. "Aye Stink!!"

"What?!" he yelled from downstairs.

I stood at the top of the railing and yelled back, "Where Diamond at?"

"She left."

"Left? Where she go at?" I asked.

"Shit, I dunno."

Heading back to my room I finished getting ready. I needed to be on the road. I ran down the stairs and grabbed my keys. Khalil was playing the game when I passed. "Aye! Where you going?" he asked.

"Around da way. I gotta pick up something."

"I'm goin.' " He volunteered himself.

I was going to debate but decided against it. Couldn't keep him in the house anymore. Looking at him my eyes narrowed. He smirked. "You already know," he said lifting his shirt showing me his Teflon vest. He knew I didn't play when it came to safety.

Making it around the neighborhood it seemed normal to the blind eye. Didn't drive my car. It was still in the shop. Seen Cortez' car and parked behind his. I knew it was safer around him. He wouldn't let nobody act crazy. Him and Khalil together I was secure.

Still was waiting on the information from Diamond, but she wasn't anywhere to be found. Called her a few times, no answer. Figured she was with a "john."

Looking up the street, Cortez was leaning on a wall, pistol in hand. He saw me, smiled, then waved us over. I gave him a hug, Khalil dapped him up. Talking, giving him the reason for me coming outside today. This little white boy walked up. I had to look hard to remember who he was. It hit me. Zach.

He went to school with us back in the day. The only whiteboy in our school. Long, curly blonde hair and looked like the little girl on the Little Debbie snacks cake box. After somebody called him that once, it became his new name. He had a chipped tooth in front of his mouth that looked like someone broke it in half perfectly, then let him keep the rest.

No matter the weather or season he wore a fuzzy grey wool cap. He never seemed to take it off. I swore it stunk. Funniest thing about him was his attitude. Acts like the world owes him. My opinion, he's an aggressive panhandler. The only whiteboy I've heard openly call a black person a "nigga." Meant it too!

He was agitated when he walked up. "Nigga! You better take this shit back, bitch! This ain't no fuckin' fifty!" My eyes bubbled with surprise.

That little whiteboy was quite the character. After getting his ass whooped four or five times all the guys around the neighborhood respected his gangsta and let him live. Basically, gave him a pass. I've actually witnessed two of the beatings. He got messed up. Never called the police. He would clean up and come right back and continue to purchase.

A real junkie, young in his career. As far as drugs, it wasn't too much that he wouldn't or didn't already try. Cortez had a screw face. "Aye lil' Debbie, if you don't get the fuck! I ain't sell your ass shit!"

Debbie scratches his chin. "Oh, my bad. You know you niggas all look alike, you know." I shook my head. That was Debbie, it was to be expected. "But uh, can you help me out?"

"What you want whiteboy?"

"I'm just trying to come up with ten dollars to get me a lil "piece."

"A piece of what?" Cortez was confused. I wasn't. I know about this epidemic the government put on the streets. Debbie was talking about K2, Spice, and all that other stuff like it. It had a hold on all the smokers, no matter what your choice was.

"A piece of deuce, nigga. My partner let me hit it with him earlier and it's like heaven wrapped in a blunt," Debbie said smiling. Cortez wasn't convinced so he continued. "You know, like how them big booty jungle girls have y'all—"

SLAP!

"Ahhh! Damn. You ain't have to hit me like that."

"Shut up cracka!" Cortez inhaled a cigarette. "I need to get some of that shit. But you know what, since I fucks wit' your dirty ass, I'ma give you twenty. Next time you come around here with your hand out, make sure you have something for me."

Debbie rubbed his cheeks, but excitement all in his face. "Thanks man. I swear I'll have something good for you."

"Yeah, I know. Let's start with dem' shades you got on. I know you stole 'em. Your bamma ass don't know shit 'bout no Ralph Lauren frames."

Little Debbie was so excited about getting high, he took the shades off quick, snatching the money, then hauled ass up the street to meet whoever.

"Crackhead ass," Cortez mumbled, then turned his attention to me. "But uh, who dis dude you 'pose to be meeting?"

I looked at my watch. "He should be pulling up any minute."

Cortez dug in his pocket and pulled out a backwoods. I'm pretty sure it was one from yesterday. he did have backwoods galore. He tossed it to Khalil who caught it and unraveled it, letting the tobacco fall out. "While we wait, might as well get litty. Pearl this." He tossed a sandwich bag to Khalil who in turn smelled it and smiled.

In my city the new one and the old one, "pearling" was what we called rolling a picture perfect blunt. It couldn't just look pretty, it had to pull just as well. Easy like Sunday morning or it would be labeled a 'fuckboy,' self-explanatory.

The blunt was in rotation and I started to feel the effects. Weed always put me on alert, but in a good way. It had a different effect on them too. Goofy. Laughing and cracking jokes. When they started talking about females, I got on my phone. I wasn't trying to hear them exchange stories. I scrolled down my contact list. I thought about calling Diamond again. Before it was possible, my phone rang.

"Hello?!"

"Uh, Naomi? I'm around here." The guy that I was supposed to meet responded.

Looked around and spotted his Mercedes. It was painted metallic black. I could tell it was armor plated. He meant business. "I see you. I'm walking to you now."

Walking toward his car a voice stopped me. "Cortez."

"Aye! Is that him?" I put my hand up indicating for him to stop.

"Yeah, it's him. I got it. If you come, he'll get spooked."

They both nodded but stayed a close distance. Just in case. Walking to the car, the back window opened. I stepped back. The guy tossed me a key, then said, "Check it out. It's in the trunk. If you satisfied toss the money in the backseat."

I looked in the backseat. Wasn't nobody there. Opening the trunk, I pulled out one long box that stretched through the trunk to the backseat, and one small box, ammunition. I smile, satisfied, and tossed the envelope full of money in the car. The window raised p and he left, leaving nothing but smoke.

CHAPTER 10

Can't even trust our own government. Especially if you a resident within the border of the Killzone. It's been time for me to go. Somewhere this city went crazy.

Driving through the streets, hands on the steering wheel and my eyes on the pavement. Lately, just been all in my mind. Thoughts everywhere. Khalil told me stop stressing. Easier said than done. It's a lot on my plate, but none of it seems to be blessing. I know I need to get it together, dying too young is not an option. Can't end up like my parents or my aunt. All she do is pop antidepressants like skittles.

Friends think I'm crazy for all the stuff I continuously keep buying to ensure safety. Rather safe than sorry. All this stress I'm under with this whole way of life, now a bounty on my life. I'm borderline paranoid, wondering why I don't do harder drugs.

I need money. Not just for me, but us. After that small caper we did, everybody gave me half to put up. Everyone agreed since

I don't have any vices, I won't pinch from it. It wasn't much compared to what we need. $1,250 was what I put up in each stash. The grand total 150,000 each. A far cry.

The funds need to start rolling in. We need bigger and badder payouts.

Think.

I know I inherited arrogance, and I'm intelligent—that's a fact. The life I living is inhumane. It's like we underground, underworld and underlined. We're the underdogs to the government were undermined. This reality isn't a once upon a time. It's really happening in real time. I have to get out of here.

BEEEEP! BEEP!

"Get the fuck out the street!" I wasn't falling for this move. I seen it too many times. Some guy laying in the middle of the street, acting like he was hurt. "Yeah, right," I said to myself.

I honked the closer I got. Instead of slowing down, I sped up. The guy jumped up when he heard my engine growl. On cue two men arose from behind the parked cars lined the street.

BOC! BOC! BOC!

I ducked beneath the steering wheel as the shots hit my car and windshield. I sped past and they continued to fire. Grabbing the emergency brake, at the corner I fish-tailed, headed down the next block. I didn't know if it was somebody responding to my bounty or just random attempt at points. Either way, I wasn't getting caught slipping. I was happy that Khalil decided to stay outside, only in that moment.

Headed home. Plans to install that electric wiring around property was in my near future. Approaching my neighborhood, the gatekeeper stood and pointed his assault rifle at my car. "STOP! Or I'll shoot!!" He took aim, inching closer.

I skidded on the brakes. "Hey! It's me, Naomi." I placed my hands out the window first, then my face so he could see me.

He recognized me. "Naomi?" He blew a sigh and lowered his rifle. "Are you okay? What happened to that car you're in?" he asked.

I got out of the car and looked. It was more holes in it than I thought. The car was smoking and sounded as if it would stall out at any moment. I looked at him and smiled. "Regular day in the city. I'm fine though."

He shook his head and stood back on post. "Well, okay, come on in."

Driving past the makeshift border, I entered my "residential area." The neighborhood was beautiful. This area always made me think of where I came from and what I wouldn't really have if it wasn't for this epidemic. Just like bums we use to stay, well not bums, but we didn't have much compared to now. Hood dudes killing each other for a better reputation and sold rock cocaine on my doorstep. This was the normal.

Khalil had a ball to bounce. I had a bike to ride and that was considered a plus. The bike didn't mean much. My mother didn't really let us play outside. Then one day my mother came home with good news. "I got a good job." My daddy did too! Financially we improved. A few months later, "Kids we moving." There was no more ducking from shotgun shells. They bought that big ass house, but really, it was an illusion. Would have thought I was "Afroman" moving to palmdale.

I didn't find out why it was an illusion until we moved. The city was now the Killzone. That's why the house was so cheap.

Pulled in my driveway. The neighborhood was quiet. Grass was green, lawn cut. Looked across the street, the same. Picture perfect. A façade.

I opened my trunk and pulled the long box out that I just purchased. The small one I tossed to the front door. Tearing through the packaging I found the instructions. It seemed basic. Straight to the point. There was a long coil of wire wrapped in a circle. The instructions informed me to wrap the wiring around the fence. Easy.

The type of fencing I had was by "Long Fence." So, wrapping it was a piece of cake. The sun was blistering today. Wiped sweat from my forehead after finishing the task. There was a fuse-type box with a power and a ground slot. After attaching the proper wires in the right spots, I needed to test it. But with what? The digital control read "live," which meant it was ready.

Exhausted, I sat on my porch. Today was a long day. I sparked a blunt, inhaled and blew a sigh. Blowing O's in the air I seen a pigeon flying. I followed it with my eyes. yeah, I was bored. It kept flying close to me. I felt like it was messing with me. It landed right in front of me and tilted his head. I tilted mines, mimicking it. The bird tilted his head the other way. Before I was about to echo it again, I shook my head. I knew I was high. I stomped at it. It flew and landed on the fence for a second before turning into floating feathers. I choked on smoke from surprise. The fence work.

CHAPTER 11

Khalil

I watched Naomi pull off after getting whatever it was that she bought online. The guy she did business with was real cautious. I understood though. You have to be this day in time. Cortez grabbed my shoulder, his way of getting my attention. "Yeah, what's up?" I asked.

"What did Nay-Nay buy now?"

"Nigga I don't know. You know she probably buying some more 'protection' type shit for the crib or herself," I said adding air quotes for drama.

Love my sister, but she is a real lunchbox. She be trippin.' That long ass box she dragged to the car looked like a rifle or some shit. That would be right up my alley. I stood on the corner with Cortez as he hustled. I wasn't really into all that. The government messed up when they told me I could carry a weapon anywhere and do as I please with it. Really. Somebody need to pray for me. I'm ready. I'm ready for whatever with whoever, forget peace. Anybody could get it with me. I'm really in these streets.

Naomi not really hip to me. She thinks I'm still that "little" brother. I'm sure she got a sample on that last caper, but really, since my folks got smoked I've been a loose cannon. My new AR-15 ready to bark. Just bought it the other day, for cheap too.

Maybe God can help. Got me killing in the city like I'm in a game. Call of duty type shit. Everybody out for self and they circle. I don't have no type. I'm out here jackin' everything. The government got me robbin' tryna' chase a crazy ass total.

One hundred and fifty thousand. Shit. I couldn't get that in regular life. My mind be everywhere. Mom dukes was a religious person. She kept us in the church for a while. I be having thoughts of heaven, thinking 'bout Hell, thoughts about freedom, thinking am I gonna prevail. But in order to do that or get that bodies need to constantly fall. I had a quota I need to meet. It's daily, wake up in the morning and ask myself, am I gonna rob today or kill? Either one gonna get me and mines on the other side of the border.

Stomach started growling. "I'm hungry, bruh," I said, rubbing my stomach, looking around for a victim or even a sweet lick.

"Tryna go to the drive-thru?" Cortez asked.

"Fuck no!" He really thinks he the Teflon don going through a drive thru. Even I done caught a few niggas loafin' on the Ave. Bullshittin'). "We could go in though."

"Where you tryna go? Micky D's by Howard?"

"Cool wit me. Let's get it," I said walking to his car.

A smile was on my face as I sat in his car. I loved his car. It sat high on the road; twenty-six inches high. It was candy painted and armor plated.

Cortez started the Caprice and the music burst through the speakers. He looked at me and smiled as he bounced to the beat. I laughed. He put the car in gear and burned rubber. The bass had the seats vibrating. The beat had our shoulders jumping. Dolby sound system cranked.

Riding up 9th Street he took Sherman Ave. He told me he had to stop around Garfield Terrace to holla at his man. It didn't bother me none. I was scrapped and so was he. We had good men around there, but still, safety first.

It was hot outside. This fool didn't want to put on no a/c. I had my shirt off, middle finger out the whip like Pac. My other hand rested on my two-tone Glock. I decided to leave the Mac-11 home today, but this Glock definitely carried enough. I was saving the AR-15 for something special at a later date.

Cortez was floatin,' foot on the gas. I could have sworn he was trying to do the whole digital dash. We neared the Battle-field, a nickname given to the neighborhood. Pulling up I noticed damn near everybody was strapped from kids to old folks. The air smelled like water, not H20 but PCP. I hoped that wasn't the reason we took this detour. I definitely didn't indulge.

The more I hung out with Cortez, the more I figured out. Parked, a couple dudes neared the car. Can't lie, I was a little nervous as I put my hand on my Glock. All I thought was two-hundred and fifty points if a nigga play.

Cortez spoke to a dude. I didn't know him, just of him. "Snake, what's up?" Cortez extended his hand. They dapped each other up. "You looking good. Seems like the statics of your money changed for the better." He smiled.

Snake shook his head. "Naw bro, but the statics of the danger remain the same 'round here."

"Yeah, I'm hip. Life's a bitch, huh? Who could you trust, right?"

"I put my faith in my Glock cause I know it gon' buss," Snake said. Even I agreed with that. Bigg facts. Glocks don't jamb.

"Yeah, I feel you bruh, but uh, you got that for me?" Cortez asked.

"Yeah, when you was pulling up, I sent my young boy to get it. Shid, I could hear you before I seen you." He giggled. "Why we waitin'? You wanna hit this wit me?"

I looked to see what he was talking about. He was putting the flame to a dipah (PCP). I shook my head as Cortez grabbed it. "Hell yeah, I hope it's Goop." He inhaled.

They chopped it up and smoked. I knew I was officially on babysitter mode. The worst. It was stamped. I leaned on the car, giving them some space. That shit stink. I heard some s hots in close vicinity. It put me on alert as I looked around with my gun in hand.

Snake peeped my vibe. "Shawty you a'ight. Ain't nothing going down 'round here unless I stay. Once you leave, you on your own." I relaxed a little.

I could tell Cortez was starting to feel the effects of the wet cigarette. A young boy came running around the building with a trash bag. He tossed it to Cortez who in turn tossed it to me. "Put it in the trunk." It felt light and fluffy. I thought it could be weed. If it was, it definitely was garbage. I couldn't smell shit!

They dapped each other up. Cortez walked toward me. He looked light on his feet. "Here." He tossed me the keys. "You drive." That's all I needed to hear. I was geeked as I caught the keys. Snake gave me a head nod and stepped off but turned right back around. "Aye Tez, you gotta come fuck wit' me like back in the day," he said.

Cortez smiled. "You my dawg til we dead, no question. But I can't fuck wit cha' like I want to cause you know what you did bruh, you a snake, Snake. I'm gone, Slim."

"I still got love for you doe, let dat ol' shit go."

I wondered what they were talking about. Something had to happen between them.

"Yeah, a'ight playa! Holla." Cortez sat in the passenger seat and looked over at me. "Hit Micky D's, Lil Bruh."

I pulled off.

CHAPTER 12

In the middle of the pavement laid a body. A confirmed kill in progress. I noticed a guy taking a picture of the body. That was the shots I heard when I was in the complex. I looked around to check my surroundings.

"Watch out for me, Tez," I said, pulling alongside the guy jumping out of the car. I pointed my gun. "Don't move a muscle! I see you in the game, huh?" I snickered.

"Please bruh, don't kill me!" He put his hands to the sky. I picked up his phone to see that he didn't send the photo. I deleted it. "You could get whateva' you want!"

"Bitch, shut up!" I looked at his choice of weapon and laughed. "Still slangin' a .380. You deserve everything I'm 'bout to give you."

"Nooo—"

BOC! BOC! BOC!

"Watch my back, bruh!" I squatted so I could get proof of both pictures. The jack body too! It's all fair fame. Fine hundred points. I'll take that.

Naomi had us all agree that money earned get split down the middle, but my body count is my own. When I say us, I mean me and my sister. Cortez and Diamond cool, but them her friends. She could split her half with them, but I need all mines.

My pops told me to take care of Naomi, not Nay-Nay and company. I took the picture and sent it to Waste Management. They were usually prompt. Momentarily, they would arrive to collect the confirmed kills and then add points to your ID.

Over the last couple of years, I raked in twelve bodies, including these two. I was halfway at the ten-thousand-point mark. Still wasn't sure where Naomi was at, far as points.

The body count in my opinion was easier to get than the money. It came with too much risk of getting killed yourself. But let her tell it, it's safer. It's what she preferred.

"Come on bruh! Follow that sign." He pointed to the big M in the sky. His face said it all. The sign must have been glowing in his mind. His smile was too big. He was smack (high).

See another car driving toward us. I took cover just in case somebody thought it was some sweet points for me. Looking in the car as it past, I noticed it was a car full of females. First though was Naomi and Diamond, especially Diamond. Persuasive. Not today. I shot a warning shot in the air. Cortez didn't blind, but the females kept it pushing. Got back in the car and pulled off.

Inside McDonald's, Cortez was trippin' good. It was comical to me. He kept feeling himself, talking about he was hot. He couldn't stay still. "Bruh, this line long as shit," he said. I looked to see it was only three people in front of us. "Fuck this." He walked to the front. "Excuse me, homies." He pushed a guy to the side. "Hey Ms. Lady, can I get —"

"Uh uh sir, there's a line." She pointed with her hips angled to the side.

Cortez looked behind. "Do y'all mind?" he asked, lifting his shirt, showing his pistol. All head shook no. "See, they don't care. Let me get a number 1." He pointed to the Big Mac Meal. "Thru twelve, yeah, and uhhh some cookies." He was dead serious as he pulled out a wad of cash. I shook my head in disbelief as he paid for it. "Bring it to the booth in the back."

Sitting in the booth I could only imagine what was going on in his head. He would smile, then mug danced to an imaginary beat in his seat. My man was trippin' good. I opened my phone from the locked screen. There was a couple of messages. One was from Naomi. Talking 'bout some gate she fixed and not to touch it. I stood up to read the rest of it. Didn't even know it was broke, but whatever. I just sent her the clapping emoji and a thumbs up. The next message made me smile. It was from my bae, Courtney.

She wasn't my girl, but we always have fun together in the streets and the sheets. She was a hitter. She wanted us to be official, but I'm not there right now. She ain't neither, but she thinks I'm not hip. I'm still tryna hit Diamond on the low. I'ma get her eventually. Courtney was gonna be my forever, but not until my play days were over. I'll never make it official.

The message, she wanted to see me. I didn't mind that, sounded like a plan to me. Only thing, I had to get rid of Cortez. Couldn't leave him like this though.

Walked back to the table to see every meal that he bought set up nicely. Burger and fries separated. Cortez just stared at it. Didn't touch any of it. I sat down. "Bruh, is you gonna eat any of it?" I asked.

"Eat what?"

"All that food, nigga! You just bought it."

"That's not mine. I ain't even hungry."

WOW

I stood up and walked to the counter. The cashier smiled before I even made it to her. "Excuse me. Could I get a couple to go bags?"

She smiled. "You friend not hungry?" she asked. I chuckled a little.

"Nah, I guess not."

"Are you from around here?"

"Yeah, why?"

"You cute, that's all."

I read her name tag. It read Stephanie. She was a pretty slim white girl. "Are you from around here?"

"Oh no! It's dangerous around here. You know, with the Killzone and all. The only reason I work here is because it pays $30 an hour. I live in Virginia."

That explained a lot. It was messed up that everybody outside the city get paid double to work. McDonald's paying thirty dollars, fuck outta here.

"So, you living in Virginia mean you can't call me or something?" I flirted.

She bit the bait. "I didn't say that." She licked her lips.

I never had a white girl before. It would be my first. Maybe hers too. She gave me the number and I saved it under snow bunny. I was definitely gonna hit her later. Stephanie gave me a couple bags and told me not to be a stranger. I blew her a kiss and stepped off.

At the booth, Cortez' face rested on the fries as he snored. LOAFIN.' I shook my head. He knew better than to be out here like that. Anytime in the streets, your head need to be on a swivel. I put all the food back in bags. When I finished, I slammed my own fist against the table.

"WAKE UP!" He jumped. Alert, as he reached for his gun.

"I'm up! What's up?"

"Shit, time to go bruh." He got up, trying to get himself together.

Leaving, Stephanie waved at me. I gave her a head nod. I was gonna call her more sooner than later. But right now, I had to get Cortez out of here.

CHAPTER 13

Wasn't too many people on the road. My neighborhood, not my 'hood, but where I lived was a one way. You would only enter and exit through the one passageway. Pulling up, old man Harry stood on guard. He already knew Cortez' car, 'SHID WHO DIDN'T?' Bright as it was.

He flagged me down and I rolled down the window. "Sup' Harry?"

He had a raspy voice like his lungs was gone. "Hey, youngster! You got any of that sticky for me?"

"Sticky?"

He loved that green, but he needed to get with the times. Nobody called it stick no more. I guess it took his mind away from the new world order. I glanced at Cortez passed out beside me. I reached over him and gave Harry a nice blunt from the glove box where I knew he kept a stash. Harry was grateful. he smiled and waved. It was the least I could do. I knew I wouldn't ever be posted up right here, so if I got it, he got it.

Arrived at the house and pulled in the driveway. The yard looked like a prison yard. It had barbed wire going through the fence. Naomi ran outside. She must have heard me pull up. "Don't touch the fence!"

I looked at her crazy. "What, we on lockdown 'round here?"

She laughed. "No, Stink! You remember that box I had earlier. This was what I bought and it's electric, so don't touch!"

"Electric?"

"Yeah, I'll give you the code when you get in here. Is that Cordy in the passenger seat?"

"Yeah, that's his high ass. High as a kite. I'm 'bout to take him to the room, but I gotta go and I'm taking his car . . . he won't mind."

"Is he cool with that?" she asked, looking dead in my eye. I smiled and she continued. "And what are you about to go do?"

"I'm 'bout to go holla at somebody. It might be a move for us later . . . oh yeah, I got five-hundred points earlier."

"You day was better than mine, but that's good as long as you were safe. But I'm also working on a move for us too," she told me as I dragged Cortez out of the car and laid him on the porch.

"A'ight, I'm gone."

"Wha What, wait! You just gonna leave him right here?"

"Yup! Your friend, your problem, Dueces."

HA

Getting in the car I decided to treat myself to a blunt as well. Whatever we had was pack! I pearled one and put the flame to it as I drove. I got on the phone and called Courtney. She answered on the first ring and the first thing she said was that she wanted to chill again. Little did she know, but I was already on my way to her.

The residents in my area thought the uptown scene was crazy. It's nothing compared to the other side. The soufside. Yes, soufside with a "F." Every block looked gloomy and smelled like death. That's where I was headed to meet her—well drive through.

At least uptown the lights and stuff still works. On this side all the lights did was flicker. Driving down Benning Road I noticed kids walking with AK's on their back like bookbags. Wasn't no cruising. I pushed the pedal to the floor and gassed it the whole stretch.

As expected, a few people shot at the car. It didn't affect me or the whip. Armor plated. I was going so fast I couldn't slow down quick enough to make my turn. I had to go around and turn on the next block. I needed to be on Central Ave. I drove damn the whole Southern Ave. To get to this side. The southside. It wasn't much different. It was still hectic over here. I was happy she lived in the cut and not in the heart of one of these hoods. Dudes around here would happily collect for my life.

I pulled in front of her house, right across the street from a firehouse. Called her and she picked up on the first ring. "Hey boo!" she spoke. "You outside?"

"Yeah."

"Come on in! It's open, my mom ain't here." I got out of my car still on the phone.

"Where she at?" Cautiously I touched my Glock as I walked in.

"I dunno! Come on, bye!"

I slid my phone close and was at her door. Opening it, the smell of something exotic rushed my nose. It was definitely pack. Sniff. Sniff. "Gorilla glue?"

Closing the door, I turned around and she jumped into my arms, kissed me blowing all gas smoke in my face. "Damn bae, let me hit dat!"

"Hit what?" She gave a seductive smirk.

"The blunt for now." She gave it to me, and I put her down turning around to lock the door. She had a bad habit of doing that. Always thinking won't nobody run up in here and get busy.

Everything was legal. I don't know what part of that she didn't understand. She stood with her hand on her hip when I turned to face her.

"I thought we was going out."

"I thought you said you wanted to chill."

"I do, but not in the house. Let's go skating." She was excited. Skating?!

Didn't really want to go there. I just was there a couple of days ago. Naomi thought I was uptown that day when really, I was on a move that went bad real quick. I still collected a confirmed kill, but no need to tell her. She worries. They both worry a lot.

Reluctantly, I agreed. "If that's what you want to do."

She folded her arm. "You act like you don't want to go."

"Not really, but for you I'll do whatever," I admitted.

"What if I tell you it's a move and we could get some money for it and a lot of it." She had a devilish grin.

On the road again, this time with Courtney in the passenger seat, looking good. She had caramel skin, light brown eyes, small but full breast and a phat ass. She had her own style which I loved. Everything she did was because she wanted to.

What I thought was a social visit quickly turned into business. She ran down the plan to me, but I needed a backdrop. During the drive she gave me some half-ass story. I blew a sigh. She funny. She had this planned the whole time. I was getting a new level of respect for her. I get it though, anything to get out, and I was with all the bullshit. I was tryna get out too.

We pulled up. She gave me a juicy kiss. "I'll meet you inside." Courtney winked.

I nodded and watched her walk inside before I exited the car.

This part was easy. All I had to do was have a good time. I entered and went straight to the food bar and ordered a pizza. Courtney glided past me with some nigga interlocked arms together. She winked at me, basically letting me know the bamma was the 'op.'

Looked like a cool dude, but in these times he should better than to trust any new bitches. They all had their own angle.

I missed my mother, she taught me so much. Females was her main topic and their manipulative ways. The power of the box she would say.

I nodded a slight nod of recognition. She skated past. I sat at the booth and sipped my 'Potion' that I snuck in and poured in one of their Styrofoam cups. Different females rolled up on me and tried their hand. Lot of them was bad, lookin' good. I would've bit any other day, but today my eyes was on a bigger payout.

I was there about an hour when my phone chimed.

'COME TO DA BATHROOM'

It was Courtney.

Headed to the bathroom her "date" walked right past me, didn't even look my way. I looked both ways before entering the bathroom. I whispered, "Courtney."

"Why you whispering?" she asked, coming out one of the stalls.

"Maybe cause I'm in the . . . never mind. What's up wit' Slim out there?"

"We 'bout to leave. This the address."

"A'ight, but what's up wit' him?" I pushed. I was still waiting on his back story. I needed to know what type of dude I was dealing with.

"Ugh," she frowned, irritated. "What does it matter?" I gave her a sideways mug. She caught my drift and continued.

"Dae Dae a real cool dude. He just started getting money. When this epidemic came through, he pulled a move and ever since then he has been on. Now he so-called balling every night, he be in that 'COME IF YOU DARE' club, throwing crazy cash around. He took an interest in me one night and since then I've been putting this in the making."

"Okay . . . and . . ." I knew it was more.

"Dang! Don't get mad, but we kicked it a couple weeks. I fucked and sucked him like a pro. I have him wrapped around my finger. He thinks he could trust me. Dumb nigga let me all in his business. I would be in the kitchen sitting down watching him break down all that white stuff. He even had me countin' his money. He swear he have a wifey on his hip. I know everything now, that's where you come in. I'm not a killer, but I know you are."

I scratched my chin taking her story in. I guess I took too long because she gave me a look. "Uhh, so what's up? He out there waitin' on me."

"Go ahead. I'm right behind you." She tried to give me a kiss. I turned away quickly and gave her my cheek instead.

"Oh yeah." She stepped back a little agitated at my demeanor. I waved her on. She smiled and walked off.

I was still stuck on that "fucked and sucked him like a pro" shit she said. I was just hoping she made him wear protection.

'YEAH, RIGHT NIGGA!'

I thought about it. I wish a broad would tell me to put a condom on for some head. I might haul off and slap fire out her. For real in this day and age I might even take the cookies for the disrespect. it is legal.

Pulled up outside the house. Didn't see the dude's car. I looked at my phone again to make sure I had the right address. It was the same. Scrolled down my contacts. I was about to text when the car pulled up. I sat low in my car and waited for them to get out. He exited the car, but Courtney wasn't with him.

'WHAT THE—'

That threw me for a loop. I watched him walk to the house. He walked to the door. Right before he knocked or could grab the handle, Courtney opened the door naked. In the same instant my phone chimed: "IT'S GONNA B OPEN."

I crept to the door and peeked in. They started French kissing. He didn't see me come through the door. She pulled him in close, leading him to the couch. She had a remote in her hand and the volume of the music increased. I didn't even think she was aware that I made it in. I could tell his head was in the clouds.

They were both on the couch as I watched him suck her nipples. I can't lie. That struck a chord. I was furious in the inside. I turned the music down and scared the shit out of him when I put the gun to his frown. "Nigga turn around. I ain't here to fuck around. You know what it is, put your hands up."

Both their hands flew to the sky. I wasn't going to do it, but I was in my body. I had to put her on blast. "Courtney that's enough. You could put your hands down." He looked dead at her and shook his head at her. I smirked. "Don't worry homie, you'll get a chance to get back once we leave with that money we after." I lied, but Courtney believed me as I read her expression.

He was livid. "Bitch, I'ma kill you!"

I grabbed his face with the gun on one side of his cheek. "Shut your mouth before I put another hole in it! Let's get one thing clear. One thing fuck in straight. Fuck your feelings! Where dat money at, fuck all that!"

Courtney responded instead. "Boo, I told you I know where everything at. Come one, we don't need him. You can go ahead and put some led in his head."

DAMN.

I looked at Dae Dae. "Pussy, right? Came out of one and set up by one."

BOC! BOC!

"A'ight come on boo!"

"Hol' up. I need these points too! Smile," I said to the corpse and the phone flashed. Confirmed kill.

After leaving the photobooth, I ran up the steps two at a time. Entering the room, she was already filling up a duffle bag full of cash. It looked like more than it probably was. Wasn't any coke, but it was plenty of weed. I took it all. Didn't care, two hundred and fifty points and some cash, I won. We bagged everything up. I sent the photo when we finished and headed back to the car.

In the car she was excited. "Did I come through or what?"

I was proud of her. She said she didn't kill. 'HA' She must have meant anymore. I remember about a year ago I had a beef with a nigga. Me, I'm on sight with mines. Seen my victim on one of our early dates. He entered a restaurant. I parked and told her to keep the car running.

Moving on emotion, I burst into the establishment. He seen me and took off. He ran through the kitchen. I gave chase. He ran out the back door. A few moments later I came through the same door.

Little did I know Courtney got out of the car right behind me. Instead of following me she went through the alley. All I seen was smoke from the silencer of her gun that I didn't even know she had. She even let me collect on the confirmed kill. 'I miss that version of her,' I thought as we cruised back to her crib.

CHAPTER 14

Naomi

Started to get irritated. The more I thought about it, the more I realized I was already there. Haven't seen Khalil in two days. Cotez been here since Khalil dropped him off. He had Cortez's car, so he was keeping me company. It was fun in all, but my thoughts were on Diamond. I know Khalil was okay. He would answer his text, but not the phone.

Diamond told me we were supposed to meet a guy about the information on my bounty. She been MIA though. Getting high and sleezy with Cortez was like rolling the dice. Either it got me tired or horny. he almost got some last night. He did get to taste it. I smiled envisioning the wonders of his tongue. Tongue game was crazy.

If it wasn't for us not having any condoms, he might've tricked me out of my panties. I couldn't with him. He knew me too well. I hated that I was like putty in his hands.

In my bedroom Cortez kept messing with me. "Boy, stop!" He kept trying to kiss my neck as we laid on the bed watching TV. I knew that my coochie was getting wetter by the second. Luckily, I was saved. It was bittersweet. THIS BITCH.

Diamond finally walked her happy go lucky self in my room, unannounced. I forgot that I gave her a sensor to disable my alarm. "I knew it!!," she raised her voice. How she said it was like a woman catching her boyfriend cheating. "Y'all ain't have to lie to me, especially you," she said. The "you" was directed at Cortez.

Cortez jumped out of the bed with a chub in his shorts, grabbed his pants and looked at Diamond. "Damn, hata', you fucked up an exotic moment in the makin'," he smirked.

"Shut up, Nasty!" I screamed on him. "You wasn't about to get none." I rolled out of my bed exposing my ass only covered by the nothingness of a thong.

Diamond smacked her teeth. "Um, I can't tell."

"Whatever!" I waved her off as I put my pants on. "But uh, where the hell you been? I hope you got some info for me," I pressed.

"Um hmm, maybe." She rolled her eyes.

Her attitude didn't make sense to me. I didn't want to dig too deep, so I brushed it off. "Well . . . spill it!"

She walked to my door. "Get in the shower. You have a date." She looked at Cortez.

He laughed like he had some understanding of her attitude. He shrugged his shoulders. "That's fine. I'm 'bout to roll anyway. Khalil 'bout to come through in an hour any minute now."

I looked at Diamond. "What was all that for?"

"Nothing. You just make sure you clean that desert up down there." She nodded to my crouch.

"Bitch, this a juice box and nothing happened for your information," I said, then slammed the door.

The water felt good hitting me as the soap ran down my body. Next to an orgasm there's no better feeling. After about fifteen minutes in I got out. Real quick compared to my usual. Anxious to meet this guy I hurried up. Put on some sexy panties and a matching bra. My outfit was basic. She said a 'date' but I didn't plan on fucking nobody. I'll leave that up to her. I just need information.

Turning the corner of the stairwell Diamond was waiting impatiently on the couch as she aggressively texted. Looking up she noticed me and stood up. Face balled up. "Bout time, hefa!" I waved her off and went to my security box and entered the code.

After the last digit was pressed, I glanced at her. "Ready?" She walked to the door, not even responding to me. I chuckled to myself. She was doing the most right now.

It was time to go. In the driveway she got in the car. My car. It was finally fixed and now armor-plated. Diamond volunteered to pick it up for me. This was my first time seeing it. It looked wider and heavy. Describing it, I'll say it was a BMW Tank Coupe, camo paint per my request with five percent tint. WAR READY.

She wanted to drive. Cool. I didn't mind, but she needed to fix that attitude she had and stop directing it at me. I didn't do anything to her. We pulled off into the sunshine. It felt good today. Here and there I would glance at Diamond as she drove, waiting for her to say something, but it never came. I broke the ice. "What's the move?"

Her eyes cut my way narrowed. "Bout to meet this clown and hopefully get some vital information." She was throwing big shade today.

I turned the music up and vibed to the tunes. "Finally." I blew an exaggerated sigh of air. Diamond looked at me after putting the car in park. "Okay, listen hookah'. He got information, but you have to earn it. Don't ask about it until the end. Whatever you willing to do he is with it. Just keep in mind the mission is information, okay?"

I looked at her like she was crazy. "What you do? Trick me out or some shit?"

"Girl, you better go get that money and information. I'm right behind you."

"Where you going? You leaving?"

"Going to the store right quick. Five minutes and I'll come in and help. Double the pleasure, double the fun." She winked.

"Whatever, slut!" I slammed the door and walked to the hotel room. Nerves was high, but I needed to know who was tryna get me killed.

HERE I GO . . .

CHAPTER 15

Diamond

Diamond. My daddy named me that for a reason. I'm flawless. I had to have the best of everything. It's my destiny. That's my middle name too! Just sayin.' Diamond Destiny Johnson. I've lived uptown my whole life. My daddy in prison and my mother will be back soon. I'm full of jokes and laughter. I think I'm still the same, but since that Bill passed, I've been turnt.' The Bill by itself could turn a kitten into a tiger, real quick.

It's a get down or lay down type world. Well, the world I'm living in. The Nation's Capital, but in our terms, The District of Corruption. It had the perfect name. Shid, I knew I was corrupted.

I was having a good day until I walked in on Naomi in the bed with Cortez. I knew she liked him or whatever, but she so damn timid and scared, she never approached him. It was like she was stuck in the past with a schoolgirl crush. She took too long, and I moved in. Me and Cortez been fucking for a couple weeks. Naomi seemed to always get the best of everything, and I was tired of it, been tired of it. For once I beat her, I was first. It happened about three weeks ago . . .

Chilling uptown it was getting late. Instead of going all the way to Naomi's house we went to his trap house. He tricked me. He knew my choice of poison, Hennessy. Cortez asked could we try something new and licked his lips.

'UM, HIS LIPS'

The drink had me feeling right. The way he whispered in my ear and licked my inner lobe with each word, I felt like I was going to lose my mind. Next thing I knew he was sexing me crazy. I mean twirling and spinning me. My head kept on spinning and my legs kept on shaking. I was twisted out of my mind, but that didn't stop me from still sipping. He had me wanting to make us something official.

Cortez knew what he was doing. Sexing me from the side, no better feeling. I was in a trance, throwing it back again, and again. He had me screaming and yelling his name. Ooh I needed him. he kissed on my thighs, then he ate it. He paused for a second and looked at, then I let him beat it.

Couldn't nobody tell me anything. I was loving that ride, smooth like his Caprice and even smoother than the henny we were drinking. Speechless is how he left me.

So, for me to see him and Naomi, I was in my feelings. I knew what he could do. She can't never let me have anything. It's okay. She will get what she deserves.

Pulling off I went to the gas station to get some cleaning supplies.

I had another money move that I needed to prepare for after I left Naomi. I parked directly in front of the gas station. There were two guys in the store already at the counter watching the Keno screen. When the door chimed, their heads turned simultaneously and stared as I walked. One of them finally built the nerve to say something when I walked down the aisle.

"Dayum you lookin' good shawty. Any room in dem jeans for me?" Cute. I smirked. I didn't even look back.

Kept it moving and ignored his advances. he had to come better than that. Still, I was cautious. My outfit for today was a long sleeve halter top with some open thigh jeans that I converted into shorts with some slight heels. Bad bitch.

Couldn't nobody tell me nothing. Walked through the aisle grabbing the necessary items and brought it to the counter. The clerk was handsome but looked too soft for me. I smiled and paid the balance. The two guys lingered, kept trying to shoot their shot. Little did they know, but if they stepped outside, I was gonna spank they ass, five hundred points for me.

The thought made my smile remain as I sashayed out the store wishing to God, they followed being thirsty. Today was supposed to be a busy day. First in line was this quick job with Naomi, then it's off to get some solo paper until this big payday come to cover a lot of money I'm about to lose.

Making it to the hotel, thoughts of Naomi being too stuck up came to mind. Her bougie ass. Didn't think she had it in her to make this money. She talked a good game, but I know the truth. Pretty soon the pieces will fall in place.

She the one that said she wanted to get down with what I was doing, so happily I set it up. Okay, so maybe I told a little white lie about who the guy was just to get her to agree. Had to, if I didn't, she wouldn't have come.

Naomi thought all she had to do was flirt and maybe dance, but this guy wanted to eat the pie. I told her when she done, he'll give her the information she seeks, but in all actuality the guy was just a trick.

At the door of the hotel room, I slid my keycard. The light turned green, granting me access. Grabbed the door handle and pushed it down. Coming in the room I heard moans. 'I KNOW THIS HEFA DIDN'T . . .' I followed the sound toward the bedroom, opened the door softly to see Naomi on top of the client, riding him like a bull. I stood in the doorway and smiled. "Damn Nay-Nay! Look at you really enjoying the op.' Did I interrupt?"

The guy was shocked, maybe scared. I did have my pistol in hand. He pushed Naomi to the floor hard and stood up with a full erection.

"What the fuck is goin' on?!"

I didn't even answer him. I was too busy laughing at Naomi getting off the floor. She was livid. Just full of surprised today. First Cortez, now the client. I knew she was a little whore.

Naomi stood ass naked. "No, this bum ass nigga didn't!" Her hair was wild, face looked crazed. Had a feeling what was to come. She looked at me. "Give me your gun, Diamond!"

I was in a trance, really, I couldn't take my eyes off a tattoo that I never seen. It was on her back and stopped at the upper part of her ass. I blew a sigh, shaking my head, walking toward her. "Here, don't do nothing stupid."

"Like what? I'm just about to ask him some questions." She pointed the gun at the client. "Who put the fuckin' bounty on me?" I smiled. he looked confused.

"Wait, what? I ordered a good time. I don't know anything about a bounty. I don't know you. I'm not even from around her. I just want sex."

Naomi looked at me but kept her aim on the client. I reminded her. "Don't do nothing stupid."

"What? Like this?"

POW! POW! POW!

I jumped back and threw my hands in the air. "Come on, Nay-Nay." I walked to the corpse. "You didn't even get the money."

She tossed the gun on the bed. "Are you serious!" She grabbed a pillow and threw it at me. "You lied to me you little hoe. Do you even know where or who put this bounty on me?"

"I'm really working on it, but look at the bright side, you earned 200 points. Be happy, boo."

"Fuck you!" she screamed.

She rolled him over, checking all his pockets, taking everything of value. Taking her phone out of her purse she snapped a picture of the confirmed kill.

Naomi wanted to go home. I happily took her back. She was a little mad, but I didn't care. made it to her house and dropped her off. She told me she was staying in and I could keep the car. "Bye hookah!" I waved.

"Try to find out something," she said as I pulled off.

CHAPTER 16

Cortez

This life is like a game that I play. I'm up from a.m. to a.m. No loafin' (slipping). I'm steady, stacking this paper. I'm tryna get the hell up outta the city. Well, at least until it's back to normal. From time to time I find myself wondering if I could even go back to the regular way of life.

Putting on a gun is a part of my regular 'fits. Without it I feel naked and vulnerable. I've done so much dirt it don't even feel like dirt anymore. It's normal. My gateway to hell is constantly opening. The reaper be calling. People wonder why I'm constantly smoking.

Being high, no better feeling. Friends of mine say I be lunchin' when I feel sexy. I just say I'm doin' me. Getting high, getting money and racking up on my body count so I could disappear.

The world knows once they granted that bill that any real nigga was gonna be a thug forever. You can't just turn this shit off. Even if I did leave, they could take me out the ghetto, but it won't make it any better.

It was a good Friday. Cruising, I was headed to my neighborhood. Just came off with some work. Diamond dropped it off to me and asked if I move it and break her off. That's easy. My clientele list is heavy. I even sell it cheap, why not, when most times I don't even pay for it.

Don't know what that sneaky lil' bitch did to get it, but I got it now. I'm glad Diamond's snake ass is on my line. She done tripped a lot of dudes up. Her box is out of this world, but I could never wife her. Now Naomi, that's my mission. Best friend in all, but I'm still tryna smash. I was close a couple days ago. She gonna love me tomar.' A thought.

Grinding, I'm trying to be a rich nigga, shine like a rick nigga, riding 'round the city every day. Riding with my window down wishing that a fiend flag me down and continue to get paid. Gonna be hitting all the bad bitches in every hood. When they come around to see me, they know I'm tryna make their body break.

It kicked in. Popped a little molly. Now I'm feeling real weird, like I'm floating on a wave.

"Brah! Why you driving so damn slow?!" Khalil looked irritated. "You throwing me off."

Forgot Khalil was even in the car with me. This shit I'm on is torch (better than rest). Just looked over there and wasn't nobody in the seat where he sat now. "Chill lil' nigga. If I speed, the police gonna pull us over." He act like there isn't a speed limit. I'm dirty as shit (got illegal products) and I don't have time for the law.

Noticed Khalil looking at me crazy. "Police? Nigga ain't no damn—you know what? You right." He shook his head and turned the music up. "Lunchin' ass nigga." I heard him mumble.

I didn't pay him no mind. I was on point. We made it around the way, and I parked. Got out of the car and didn't even feel like I was walking. I was happy. Knew I felt good. Cheeks were hurting from smiling too hard, I guess. Felt like the cartoon when they following a scent with their nose high, but legs bent at the knees as they floated.

Khalil hated when I was litty', but even on my worst I'm always on point no matter how high I get. All I do is dream big. Go big and go hard.

"What the fuck you over there talking about?" Khalil asked with what sounded like irritation.

I looked at him. "You ain't even got to talk to me like that. You hurt me, right here." I pointed to my chest. He waved me off.

"What's da move then?" he asked.

Didn't have any plans for real. Hustle, chill. I knew Khalil didn't hustle, but I was open to any and all moves. We smoked a blunt and just kicked it. Khalil was high. I was higher. Down the street I followed Khalil's eyes to see what he was looking at, my favorite little white boy.

"Ain't that Debbie right there?" Khalil asked.

I smiled and answered him. "Why yes, it is." Anytime he came it was some for sure bullshit attached. Sometimes he come with something valuable. I always wondered how he was still alive. I guess the ten points wasn't worth it. Why waste the bullets.

Zach, aka Little Debbie, made it closer and extended his hand for some dap. His preppy white boy voice made me laugh every time when he spoke. "How's is going, niggas?" I smacked his hand down. "Always hatin' on a brother." He looked at Khalil, gave him a head nod. "Wakonda, what's up?"

Khalil looked at me, then pointed to Zach. "Get you mans, bruh." His face tight.

Zach looked at me and raised his hands. "No beef, no beef. But uh, Cortez, why you look like that?"

"What! I know you ain't joinin' (crackin' jokes) wit' your slow lookin' ass, dirty white holes in your sock lookin' ass." He tried to cut me off, but nope. I cooked his ass.

"Shut up wit your rat lookin ass. This your brain on drugs lookin' ass!"

Khalil couldn't stop laughing. Zach was silent, just for a second. He knew I fried his no eyebrow can't blink lookin' ass. He was used to it though. After the laughter Zach got serious.

"Hey, remember I said I'd bring you something good?" I nodded. "Well, I got some info for you. It's a move, something I know y'all like, but you have to break me off a lil' something." Zach smiled.

I was skeptic, but my curiosity outweighed it. "Go ahead Debbie, I'm listening."

"Because y'all my niggas," Khalil inhaled, rolling his eyes. "I mean my friends," Zach corrected, noticing Khalil getting offended. "I know this spot where there is plenty drugs and money."

Khalil interrupted. "How you know 'bout this so-called move?" A crazy look plastered his face as if he didn't believe a word. I don't blame him. This could be a set up, but that cracka' wasn't crazed. I still needed more convincing.

Zach spread his arms. "Come on, have I ever lied?" My facial expression answered for him. "That was different, but to ease this nig—, I mean, this strong black man's suspicions. I was working at his house. I installed a few deadbolt doors and walked past a room where I noticed a big table with three money counters and piles of money. The guy in charge name was uh, Pretty P—"

"Pretty P?" I asked.

"Yeah, you know him?"

"Yeah, I do."

"So, you know I'm not lying! After I fixed the doors they were talking, so I stood by the door listening. I think one of his homies plan on back dooring him at this party tonight."

"What was said?" I was interested. Back dooring was my specialty.

"Okay, listen. This guy Sean, who is Pretty P's friend, is the snake. he set up a buy, but Sean plan to rob him for it all. It's a big order. He said if all goes well, he would be "super straight," and be the man. But if you come in and crash the party, you can get the money and drugs. So . . . Did I do good? I'm only telling you because I know how y'all get down and plus I'm trying to look out for y'all because I know y'all gonna look out for me."

Khalil was shaking his head. "That's why I don't let nobody in my house. You one of the reasons Naomi be putting all that shit in the house."

After listening to Zach give the whole rundown, I decided to call Naomi. I knew she would want some of this money. Khalil and I devised a plan. Little did I know, but Zach left out a small fragment of information that I would soon find out.

Naomi pulled up. Surprisingly, she was in an Uber. The car didn't look familiar when it arrived. I almost put a few holes in the driver. The only thing that stopped me was that she was white. Didn't need that beef. She was a restricted employer. Inside her car, she safe.

Naomi got out of the car looking like G.I. Jane in her fatigues. It was sexy. My joint jumped when I noticed how tight it fit around her ass, bubble ass at that.

DAMN I NEED DAT!

She tilted her neck. Caught me staring. "Ready?"

"Uh, yeah. My bad, let's go."

This type of move I couldn't drive my car. It's pretty noticeable, so I had to take somebody else's. I knew Pretty P—well, knew of him. Wild lover, he wasn't your average hustler. Spending fifteen years in the penitentiary had changed his perception of life. He was tall, a tall light skinned dude with good hair. Weighting in about 240 solid with muscles on top of muscles. He wasn't to be taken lightly. The only thing that had me stay away from him was he was a faggot. He was on cheeks hard as shit. In the hood we call them homo-thugs by day. Bust guns and get money. By night he was bussing down boys left and right.

I wished he would have taken a different route. I would've been getting money with him, but rumor has it that if you worked for him you had shared a piece of yourself with him. I'm not rockin.' Not in the cards. Not never. This day in time you wake up, you winning, so who am I to judge.

Leaving T Street, making a left on Seventh, we headed up Georgia Avenue. Damn near drove the whole avenue. I was close to Silver Spring, about a few blocks from the station and border.

A big white house with green shutters was the description given. Sixteenth Street, almost like a suburban neighborhood with mansions. As we rode past the house, I noticed the garage wasn't completely closed. Just enough space to squeeze under.

From the outside the party looked to be in swing. It was colorful lights flashing. I parked two houses up and we walked down a slight hill. Once at the house we crawled under to gain access.

Inside the garage we pulled down our masks, turned around to look at Naomi and Khalil. "Ready?" Khalil nodded. Naomi chambered a round. "On the count of three. 1, 2,—"

"Wait!" Naomi stopped me before I kicked the door. She turned the knob and to my surprise it was unlocked.

Quietly turning the knob, I was on Naomi's heels. "Boy, back up!" she whispered. I got a free funky roll. "10 points!"

"Shut up!"

I heard voices. Bitches?! They were singing in unison. As we crept, the music and the voices got louder. "Biiitch! Turn that uuppah. That's my song!" she sang a Beyonce anthem. 'GET MY BODY'

What sounded like a group of girlfriends getting their party, turned out to be the complete opposite. There was a group of dudes in the middle of the room, twerking and singing Beyonce. I was shocked. "Maaan, fuck nah!" I threw my hands in the air almost forgetting my reasons for being there.

The dudes heard me through the music and turned straight toward us. One of them acted like we didn't have guns pointed.

"Uh, uh! Who da fuck let y'all in?"

Khalil laughed at the sound of the gump's voice. He stood still with his hand on his hip, awaiting an answer.

"Deez nuts, now y'all get the fuck on the ground before I make you!"

All of them hit the floor except one, the one. The boy had heart. "Nicca fuck you! Ms. Peaches don't get on the ground for nobody, but Pretty P."

BOOM! BOOM!

I flinched, as Ms. Peaches hit the ground.

Looking back was Naomi with a smoking barrel. Khalil smiled and said, "That's my cue." He jumped over Ms. Peaches' lifeless body and headed straight upstairs.

The house was huge. Me and Naomi was about to split up until I heard the garage open. One of the boys lifted his head up. "Pretty P here! Y'all fucked up now."

"Shut up, bitch!" I hit him with the side of my gun. I ran to the wall and turned the lights out. The door opened from the garage.

"Daddy's home! Where my bitches?" He yelled joyfully.

"Heellp!" a voice screamed.

Pretty P turned the light. To his dismay he stared at a pistol rested on his temple. His homie stood beside him, shocked as well. Sean, I'm guessing.

Naomi had her cannon pointed at him. I decided to play a game. "Sean, is this him?"

Sean looked confused. Pretty P looked at him with venom in his eyes. Sean tried to explain. "Homes, I don't know this nigga."

I frowned my face. "Damn, slim. You told me he da the plug. But since you acting funny, I'ma leave you wit his ass."

"Hold up!" Pretty P said. "I'll give you whatever, if you let me live and kill that nigga myself." He eyed Sean.

I smiled. "Okay, you convinced me. I can tell you really mean that. Let's go Casanova, off to da safe! All of them too. Sean told me everything. Nay-Nay! Watch them. If they sneeze, 250 points each." She smiled.

I escorted Pretty P to each and every safe. It was three of them. This was a helleva payday. Drugs and money. I wondered to myself why he still stayed in the city. I relieved him of two keys of cocaine and $150,000 cash. He had a ticket out, but didn't cash in. Then I understood. Why leave? Everything you want to do is legal. Survival of the fittest. That earned him some relief.

"Listen freaky slim. I'm not gonna smoke you. But them nigga bitches downstairs, them bitches dead. I'ma let you smoke your man. he a snake and I hate those."

He blew a sigh. "Respect."

CHAPTER 17

Naomi

I needed a body in ways that nobody seemed to understand. I'm losing my patience. Somebody is trying to kill me, and I don't know who. I just want to find the culprit and get it over with. Ya know, level the playing field and get it on. I just want to make them scream. I'ma make sure that I kill him slowly. There won't be a speed limit to my confirmed kill when it's in progress. I'm gonna . . .

"Nay Nay!" Khalil called me. I was lost in my thoughts as I held my stance.

"Yeah?!"

"Where Cortez at?" he asked, looking around, then noticed the new guy. "And who da' fuck is that?"

"Some dude named Sean. He came in with Pretty P," I said matter of factly.

He shrugged his shoulders. "Oh. But uh this all I could find. I almost got lost in this bitch." He had a bag of jewels and some petty cash.

I smiled. "Don't worry, Stink. Cordy upstairs getting the rest of it as we speak."

The house was big. Khalil told me he checked like eight rooms while he was upstairs. Pretty P was living like a king. It made me wonder if he was that rich before the Killzone was legislated and if so, why was he still here?

I pulled my phone out since I had a little downtime and decided to call Diamond. It had been hard to get a hold of her lately. Not to my surprise she didn't answer. Started to think she was lying about her so-called "connect" that she supposedly knew. She already had me out of my element with that last guy. Selling my body was not my way of getting money, even though the guy laid it down. That's not me.

I refuse to let the District of Corruption change my morals and principles. Killing, that's different. It's life or death with that.

Pretty P came down the steps first. Cortez was behind him with his gun pointed, dragging a bag.

BOOM! BOOM! BOOM!

Three shots.

Three victims.

Cortez shot the remaining girls. I called them "sexy lady boys." Two of them were cute. I could tell they could easily trick the average guy. Pretty P stood back up after the shots. He had dove on the ground after the first blast let off. He shook his head as he looked at the pool of blood that formed around the bodies of his lifeless squad of boys.

Sean knew it was over for him. His face told a sad story. Cortez looked at my brother and pointed. "Aye Khalil go get dat' bag from the top of the stairs," he said, dropping the one he was carrying. he patted Pretty P on his shoulders.

"Okay, Freaky P, it's your turn." I watched him pull the clip out of his gun and pop all the bullets except for one. "Here you go, do you." Cortez gave the gun away.

I didn't like that. I pointed my gun at Pretty P's face, but asked Cortez, "What the fuck you doin,' Cordy?"

He waved me off. Yeah, he waved me off like he was some type of Teflon Don. "It's cool. It's fine. Don't even trip. If he points that gun at anything but his homeboy, blow him da' fuck up! Send 'em to tha' moon."

"My pleasure." I smiled. Pretty P knew I didn't have no problem bussin' his melon. His sexy lady boy already told him that I shot Ms. Peaches' loudmouth ass.

"Chill lady!" Pretty P said, turning his back to me, pulling the hammer back, placing the one round in the chamber. Sean tried to plead, but his cries weren't acknowledged as Pretty P spoke. "Shut up, Hoe! I gave your faggot ass the world. Now it's time to take it away."

BOOM!!

A trickle of blood rolled down Sean's forehead as the back of his head went in every direction.

"DAYUM! That was cold, Slim." Cortez grabbed the gun.

Khalil shook his head. "Nah, that wasn't cold. That shit was gay! A faggot calling a faggot a faggot. I'm ready to go."

Cortez laughed, then looked at me. "So, what y'all 'bout to do?"

The question was dumb in my opinion. I wasn't going anywhere without that money. He knew that so I don't know why he even tried to play me. Really didn't know how much bread was in there, but I wasn't about to let him leave and just break me off on his time.

'NAH, NOT HAPPENIN.'

The duffels looked heavy too! Khalil couldn't even carry the one he brung down the stairs, so I knew it had to have plenty inside.

"I'm 'bout to sit right here and see what's in dem' bags."

"You wanna do it in here?" Cortez asked.

"Uh, yeah. Why not? What you think the police on the way?" Sarcasm was evident in my tone.

He smiled. "Listen, Boo . . ." I loved it when he called me that. "It's one hundred bands in this duffle and drugs. I know you or Khalil don't want the work so I'm just gonna let you and lil' bruh split the bread. Fifty a piece and I'll keep tha' work."

He said that a little too quick for me. I knew the drugs must have been worth much more, but he was right, I didn't want no damn drugs, so reluctantly I accepted his deal.

"Give it here!" I extended my hand.

Cortez opened both bags and showed me that one held money and the other didn't. Khalil watched like a lost puppy. Probably mad I didn't give him any say so. We locked eyes. "I'll give you yours at home." I looked at Cortez. "But uh, what's up wit' ur' boy?" I nodded to Pretty P.

Pretty P was quiet as a mouse, just watching everything. I almost forgot he was alive. I pointed my gun at him.

"Ho-Hol' up lady." He threw his hands u p and put one leg in the air imitating the Heisman trophy. "I-I know you and I have some info for you if you let me live."

I lowered my gun. In unison both Khalil and I asked, "What info?!"

"I'll never forget a pretty face like yours, especially when it's a seventy-five-thousand-dollar bounty attached to the photo of you."

I leaned closer. "You threatening me?"

"N-nah. I know who put that price on your head."

"Who?!"

"You gonna let me live?"

"Yeah, of course," Khalil answered. I didn't say a word.

"That's your word, Homes? That's all we got nowadays," Pretty P said, pleading through his eyes. Khalil nodded.

"A'ight. My homeboy told me this broad he was fuckin' offered it to him."

"Fuck dat! Give me a name." I was getting agitated.

He blew a sigh. "Ruby, Robin, Diamond, some shit like that. Redbone joint, phat ass booty. I never seen—"

"SHUT UP!"

I looked to the sky. Many thoughts flooded my mind. Not my bestie. Why would she want me dead? Thoughts of the past flooded my mind . . .

Memories

Never in a million years would I have expected this. Never knew she felt any ill will toward me. Thirsty? Thirsty enough to kill me. Lost in my thoughts, a memory came to mind.

Before the Killzone and all the nonsense after it, Diamond and I was at the skating rink. It was named Crystal's. It was us and these two dudes. She knew her date, mine was a blind date. Diamond always been gutter and played with guns. Her parents were former police, and she was taught how to shoot and disassemble most weapons. She seemed to always date the bad boys as well. This particular guy was named Zeek. He was from uptown.

I called him, Big Freaky. He always tried to convince Diamond to convince me to a threesome. I wasn't into all that. I barely even had sex. On this day while we were out, her date was beefin' with some dude. The end result, Zeek beat the shit out of the two dudes as my date beat the other guy.

Just watching him fight and win solidified a place in Diamond's sheets. But for me, that day was a milestone when I just knew I had a friend to the end. Leaving the rink, we went to a nearby Bojangles to get some chicken. It was good. We sat and enjoyed our meal until it all went to shit. The guys that got beat up came back with a vengeance. Guns were blazing!

I wasn't used to that type of stuff. I was scared as shit and dived under the table. Back then I was petrified of weapons. All I heard was screams and gunshots as I covered my ears and closed my eyes. Shockingly, I opened my eyes when I felt a presence under there with me. It was Diamond holding what I now knew was a Smith and Wesson .40 caliber that she pulled from her purse.

"Shhhh! I got us, girl," she said. I crawled behind her.

One of the dudes looked under the table where we were, and she didn't hesitate. She pumped seven hollow tip bullets into his chest. He was holding himself as the bullets pierced his body forcing him to drop his extended round Glock and land on top of it.

She looked at me and winked. "You my girl for life, never forget dat'."

I blew a sigh.

"Nay Nay!" Khalil waved his hand over my eyes after I blinked a few times. I was lost in my thoughts as he continued. "You a'ight?"

I moved Khalil to the side, well out of my way as I approached Pretty P, digging into my pocket. Retrieving my phone, I entered the security code and showed him my screen saver. "Is this her?" It was a picture of me and Diamond cheek to cheek in a selfie. He nodded his head yes. My heart dropped. I was hoping he was mistaken. I didn't want to believe him. Felt like I was having a heart attack as the beats in my chest rapidly sped up. I held my chest. Wanted to get more information out of Pretty P, but what was the use. Her name alone was enough confirmation. I didn't know that dude and he damn sure didn't know me.

I was livid.

Stormed out of the house leaving everyone behind. Felt someone following, but I didn't care. Emotional. My eyes started to water. Made it outside and forgot Cortez was my transportation. My car was uptown.

"Sis, what's up?!" Khalil asked from behind me. Before I turned to face him, I wiped the tear that threatened to roll down my cheek.

"Yeah, Stink, I'm cool." I forced a smile. "We got fifty bands and a confirmed kill. We gonna be outta this shit hole soon, baby bro," I mustered up.

Really, I was . . . I don't know what I was. All I knew was that I needed to see Diamond.

Damn.

No car.

I looked in the driveway and decided to take one of Pretty P's cars. He didn't need them anymore. I figured Cortez would finish him off. Khalil jumped in the passenger seat after tossing the duffle onto the backseat.

"So, what we bouta' do," Khalil asked. "All I wanna know is could I smash her first."

"Not right now, Stink. Shit about to get real," I told him as I pulled off.

CHAPTER 18

Diamond

Today was a good day. I had to make some money today. It had to be over five thousand. I've yet to count it. I was on moves all day and everything went like it supposed to. I dumped all the money on the bed. I was at Naomi's house in my room swimming in the cash.

In the bed I kicked my clothes off. All that remained was a tiny pair of boy short panties and a tank top, no bra. Comfortable.

I tossed my wig that I had on for the caper on the floor. I'll clean up later. Even if I didn't, Naomi would do it for me. She is a neat freak. On occasion I would leave it messy just for her. I'll be chilling and trick her into coming in my room to grab one thing—next thing she'll be cleaning on impulse. Such a sweetie she is. I'm amazing, just saying.

Needless to say, I kept a check. # never broke. Reason being why I felt so exhausted, barely breathing, but definitely holding onto what I believe in. Take a guess. High potency weed graced my lungs as I laid on the bed. I needed it. Had to have it every day. Spoiled, some would say. All I know is that it always put me on my level.

Don't know if I was trippin', but I could have sworn I've been smoking this same blunt for . . . hours. This same show was on the television watching me. If it wasn't for the ash falling, burning my thigh and the TV screen turning blank, and the camera channel appearing showing me Naoli pulling up grabbing my attention, I would've still been stuck.

Was about to get up . . . Fuck it, I thought just as fast as the thought came. I was in my zone. I turned my iPod speakers on blast. The sound of the electric guitar came on first. I bit my bottom lip. This was my song. I closed my eyes as I turned the volume up. This song talked to me every time. I sang along to Rihanna's Kiss It Better:

Been waitin' on that sunshine boy I think I need dat back
Can't do it like dat, no one else gon' get it like dat
So I, argue, you here, here to take me back
Who cares when it feels like crack, when you know that you always do it right . . .

Didn't even hear Khalil come up the stairs until I saw my door swing open. He had a creepy ass smirk on his face. I turned the music down.

"Boy get out!!" I reached for my sheets to cover my body.

"Don't stop singing on account of me wit' your sexy ass," he said, moving closer. He grabbed the sheets and snatched them off my body. "Been wanting this box that you keep playin' with." He licked his lips.

"Boy if you don't . . ." I stood up. "Nay Nay! Come get your freaky ass brother before I fuck him up!" It wasn't funny anymore. He was acting weird. Felt like he was going to try me.

Naomi walked in. Crazy part she just leaned on the wall. "Do you, Stink."

DO YOU! DO WHAT?

Didn't know what they thought was about to go down. I know they wasn't on no freak shit. "Y'all trippin'. Move." I tried to walk past. My ass was out and everything. If they wanted to play, this was not funny.

Khalil stepped in front of me. he blocked my path. I looked around him at Naomi. "you serious?"

"As a heart attack," she said, as Khalil turned me to face him and punched me hard as shit. I flew on the bed. Felt like my jaw was broken.

I felt the weight of his body land on top of me. He ripped my panties off first as if it were paper. Next, was my tank top. My breast bounced after being released and I tried to crawl and kick.

"Stop!" I screamed. Didn't understand why he was doing me like this and why was Naomi letting him. "P-please . . . let me go," I begged.

Naked, on my stomach he dragged me as I kicked. He hit me again. That was it. That last punch took all the fight out of me. I laid flat, no resistance. He hit hard and I felt it.

Khalil turned me on my back. "You should have been gave me this pussy. Keep lettin' these wild niggaz smash. It's my turn."

Naomi was still on the wall. I glanced over at her one more time for help that never came. She grinned and chambered a round in a gun that I didn't see before. Turning my attention back to Khalil he pulled his massive tool out of his pants. It was huge. Too big for my liking. Thirteen inches and veiny.

My heart dropped. I knew I couldn't take all that. He bent me over and spit in my ass. I was hoping he missed when he spit, but no, he forced his tool inside my ass, splitting me open at the same time. I screamed at the top of my lungs . . .

"Wake up! Wake up!" Wayne shook me. "It's just a dream, boo," he reassured me.

I woke up panicked as I scanned the room. I wasn't in Naomi's house getting butt raped. Breathing hard I wiped sweat off my forehead. It felt so real. Never have I ever had a nightmare like that.

My eyes were wide as I stared at the wall. "She knows," I said to the air.

Wayne looked confused as he stood in front of me. "Who know what?!" he asked as I looked straight through him, a little lost in my thoughts. Too many thoughts. Different scenarios ran laps in my head. Hope for the best, but my intuition was telling me the opposite.

Maybe if someone told her, she'll never believe it. It was a hefty price on her head, maybe just maybe she thought I couldn't afford it. Little did she know, me and my mother have always been in contact since she left. I could have left with her, but not until I tied a few loose ends. Then I couldn't leave my man here, not the one beside me but Cortez. He already told me he would come with me, but to solidify it I had to get Naomi out of the way, unbeknownst to him.

Really, could've did it myself, but that would have put Khalil on the chopping block like he is now. I like Khalil too, might have even eventually let him get a taste. I knew he was geeked over this bomb pussy I got, but my instincts telling me to tread water.

I've never had a dream like that before. It had to mean something was wrong.

"Uh, bitch. I know you not iggin' me?" Wayne asked.

Come to think about it, this shit was all his fault. His idea I let this fool put the battery in my back and put the hit out. That pillow talk mean. But to be fair, I might have lied about the reasons and who it was. I even gave him false promises that we'll be together. I got plenty of love for him, but my eyes are on someone else. The best part of our relationship, other than sex was that he presented me with plenty of money moves. Truly he was oblivious to my turn up.

"First off, I'm not your bitch." I pressed his forehead with my index finger. "Secondly, we gotta go." Picking up my phone, endless missed calls. Twelve to be exact. A few from Cortez and multiple from Naomi. I blew a sigh. I hoped Cortez didn't know and if he did, I prayed he wasn't on her side, for a change.

Naomi always thought she was the best in everything, but one thing I know I have over her is my pistol game. She ain't ready.

I looked at Wayne as he put his clothes on. "Boo! I need a favor," I asked with my innocent face. He blew a sigh and narrowed his eyes.

"What?" He knew I was on some bullshit, but he couldn't deny me.

"I need you to go around 9th Street and just kick it with Cortez and try to get some info," I plotted.

"Info? What kind you talkin' bout?"

He was starting to blow me, getting me irritated as I sighed. "Tsst, just whatever he wanna talk about."

"Oh, okay. Like bitches n' shit?"

I hit him in the back of his head. "No stupid."

"Ouch." He rubbed his head. "What was that for?"

"For being dumb as a rock."

"How can I be dumb as a rock? It ain't got no brain," he said, making my point.

I hit him in his chest this time. "Ouch!"

"You stupid!"

He looked like he wanted to hit me back as he huffed and puffed. "I'm not doing shit! Matter of fact I'm 'bout to roll, 'bout to head home."

"What home nigga? You ain't got no crib. If you did then why we in this hotel?"

"For your info, I finally got my very own place where I can do what I want, when I want."

I put my hand on my hip. I didn't believe one word this fool was saying. "Where at?"

"In my parent's basement, jealous?" he said proudly, standing up. "Plus, I got shit to do. I promised my sister I'll come up to her school and give a speech." He popped his collar. "I stay busy."

"A speech?" I asked, then noticed him looking in my purse. "And what you think you're going to find in there?" I asked with confusion plastered all over my face.

"Yeah, a speech. And if you must know I'm looking for something to take the edge off before I go give the kids the 'don't do drugs talk, ya dig."

"You right, I'm done." I waved him off. "Stupid self."

"Not stupid, and it's bring your parent to school day and tell the kids your occupation."

"Oh yeah, that's what's up." I headed to the bathroom, trying to end the conversation, but he wasn't finished as he spoke to my back.

"And you can't come. You have to have a real job. An organ collector isn't an option."

A smile came naturally as I slammed the door to the bathroom. I looked in the mirror. Reality kicked back in and I had to push Wayne's retarded self to the back. Nothing was certain yet. All thoughts and assumptions from a dream. A lot of questions and no answers. I wanted to call but decided against it. My next move, undecided. I turned the shower on and got in.

CHAPTER 19

Cortez

Man. I can't even picture myself not breathing. I'm in this crazy dilemma. Diamond's not even answering her phone. Typical. But in this circumstance, I needed her to pick up the phone. I love too much. I love too many to count 'em. All this shit I be doing, I shouldn't have no close friends because they are the first my enemies would try to get a hold of. Love is extra; it seems like it would be easier to go on without it.

Everything goes away. It's worse when it's stolen away. Makes me mad. Why did it have to be so close in my circle? I already someone is going be laid to rest. I'm not afraid of death, it's the thought of my people getting laid to rest. Never would I want to see the blood of someone I love draining on the outside of them.

That would suck balls. It's a couple million ways to die. Not even this big ass blunt could fade the stress.

One thing for certain is that somebody is lurking in these streets trying to close your curtains. I'm just confused as to why it would be her. Diamond. Only assumption is that this bill turned people into something out of some dream with a devilish soul for hurting, me included.

Often, I be wishing I didn't love, but when it's away I be missing love. Like I love Naomi and Diamond maybe one more than the other and it makes it hard when in these times your mother, your brother, your sister and your father are living to die just because in this Killzone the ditch is already dug.

I get nauseous cause I can't see my death and it causes me paranoia activity which always leaves me cautious.

Crazy is how I describe the situation between Naomi and Diamond. I don't even know if it's true. people would do and say anything to save their own life. For example, Pretty P didn't work in his case, but it was a good effort, I guess. Definitely smoked his ass though, ol' freak nigga. Bamma talking 'bout I promised him I wouldn't kill him. "Nigga I ain't say no shit like dat." I remember her saying . . .

"Bu-but your folks said I was good if I told her about the bounty." Pretty P tried to refresh my memory of what Naomi promised him. Didn't really care about what she said or didn't say. Her ass was up and outta there, so whatever she said left with her. All the bitch come out of dudes when that pistol in their face. This gangster ass punk was really begging like the bitches that laid dead on the floor.

Bitches, I laughed to myself thinking of Naomi. She called them "sexy lady boys."

Really, I didn't want to kill him, but how could I not. Couldn't let him live, then let him regroup and put a bounty on me. He definitely had the funds and the contacts to make it happen.

"Nope, don't recall saying that. Heard it but didn't say it. Come to think of it she delivered you're breathing and she gone. But she can't speak for me," I said, raising my pistol.

He swallowed hard.

I smiled hard.

That confused him for some reason. I noticed his demeanor change. He was relaxed. He had to have thought I was going to let him go. That was false and a bad assumption on his part.

Random thoughts. I was smiling, thinking how I'm about to be all the way on after I get this money from this flip. I didn't know what he was thinking. He turned toward me, took a step closer. Nigga had to have just grown a set of balls. His face turned into the meanest mug I've seen in a long time. If I didn't know the truth, I might have believed it.

"Do what you gotta do, homes. I know the rules to this shit when I signed up," he said, stepping closer.

I tilted my head to the side as he talked and tried to get closer. "Niggas gonna remember me. I'm dat nigga—." Boc!

Headshot.

"Hmm." He got too close. I got too nervous. The end. Wasn't about to have no wrestling match in here over my gun. Really wanted to squeeze him, have a little fun getting some info out of him, but his head attacked the bullet in my gun. It was really a tragedy. I had the work, now it was time to ghost this spot, but not before I get proof of all these confirmed kills.

"Say cheese!" One by one I snapped away.

Contemplating my next move, I was about to leave, but why? Pretty P dead. His flock left before him. I didn't have nowhere to go.

"Mi casa su casa," he once said.

Since he gone it's mines. I tossed the bag on the floor and began dragging each body to the sidewalk. Waste management would be here any minutes. They were always quick and on time.

Inside the house I had free reign. Call it what you want, it was shopping time, and everything was free. I headed up the stairs to what I knew was my new bedroom.

The walk-in closet looked like a clothing store in its own right. I slid the door open, and it led to another room. The way Pretty P had it arranged gave the illusion of a regular closet, but the back wall was knocked out, leading to the room on the other side. Now it was just one big ass closet/room.

'RICH ASS.'

He had everything and it was all to my liking. Rummaging through the clothes, I found an outfit for the day. I tossed it on the bed and headed to the shower.

'NICE.'

Everything was marble and pearl. Real clean and new. Inside the shower was a control panel. That was some new shit to me.

'FUCK DA HANDLES AT?'

I guessed the panel controlled the blasters I seen surrounding me. It was about fifteen of them. I hit the regular settings and decided to play with the other options later. A quick five-minute shower was all I took.

Standing in front of the floor mirror in my new shower robe by Gucci, I lotioned up.

'I COULD GET USE TO THIS.'

So many selections. I opened a cabinet and seen nothing but different fragrances. A lot. I grabbed the Polo and dapped a few drops on my neck and wrist. It smelled so good that I knew once the broads see my new look, my pussy rate gonna skyrocket.

After putting on my new clothes I exited "my" house. The bodies that I stacked on the front were gone and a receipt was on the door. "Confirmed kills." I smiled.

I hit my alarm to my car, then looked to the left. There was a Tesla in the driveway. I smiled again.

'I'LL DRIVE THAT.'

I pulled my Caprice into the driveway and stretched out in the spacious Telsa. Never drove one before, now I have one of my own. I pulled off.

CHAPTER 20

The drive was cool. Relaxing. Guess it felt good when you know that you just came up and about to be super straight. My mind was on me. Team me. Naomi and Diamond's situation was a distant second thought, making its way to the back of my mind. Don't get me wrong, I was thinking about it, but this money kind of outweighed thoughts of them.

The Tesla was the truth. Everything advertised about it was facts. It even drove itself if you wanted it to. Never was gonna enable that feature, but it was still like that. I parked around my way, got out and just admired the car. When I was driving through everybody showed love.

DAMN YOU SEXY.

I ran my hand down the car as I walked to the trunk. With a push of a button, it lifted open so I could retrieve my backpack.

I had to pinch off a few grams that I was gonna sell hand and hand.

Today was gonna be a good one. I could feel it. Everything must go. I might even have a two for one crack give away. I smiled at the thought. I was kinda mad that Pretty P didn't have no trees in that big ass house. All I had left was about 7 grams of Gorilla Glue I got from the weed man around the corner. I rolled a blunt and posted up.

Head on a swivel.

That's a must.

I noticed a car on a slow, but moderate creep. Instinctively my hand reached for my Glock before I even seen the driver and/or passengers. Nigga wasn't gonna get a payday off me. That's dead, my thoughts.

Had to walk away from my car and lean on somebody else's. Didn't want my new ride to get riddled with bullets. There was me, the parked car, then the street. Coverage. I watched the car near.

Glock in hand as I narrowed my eyes tryna see into the approaching vehicle. The driver was smart. He lowered his window before he got too close.

Ready.

Geeking to buss but didn't.

The face looked familiar. It was my nigga Wayne. He wasn't my man man, but he was cool. He was from Clifton Street. We went to school together. Haven't seen him in a while, especially since this new way of living was introduced into legislation. Dudes just don't cruise around other neighborhoods anymore.

I kept my hammer on my side just in case. We didn't have any beef or anything like that, but still didn't know what he could have wanted.

He pulled up and parked. By himself, which was a plus, it semi-mellowed me out and I dropped my guard. "Big Tez!" He was excited as he spoke. "What it do baby?"

I smirked at his animation. "Shit, getting money so I could get the fuck one day."

"That's the move we all tryna accomplish, ain't it?" He grinned. "But I ain't doing shit. You know my lil sister go to the school around da corner. I just left her, now I was just cruzin'."

"Dats what's up. You a'ight?"

"Yeah, coolin'. I'm a lil faded," he confessed. "You should have seen me in that school tryna give a damn speech about not doing drugs when I was high my damn self." He chuckled.

"You crazy ass shit, Slim. Fuck you on now?"

"Prescription pills. I'm rollin' boots right now."

"Tryna smoke?"

"Fuck yeah. Hell yeah! Fly dat shit in." He leaned on the car. "You ain't seen Diamond wit her phat ass? I've been tryna catch up with her."

Can't lie. I was a little tight when he asked about her. I played it natural. "Nah. I'm looking for her too. Her sneaky ass, I'm tryna get in her ear tight now about some whole other shit," I said, keeping it short.

"Fuck she do now?" He looked too interested, but I didn't pay it no mind as I responded.

"Don't know but been hearing some wild shit. The shit throwing me off."

"Like what?" he asked.

None of your damn business, I thought.

"Don't trip, but what's up wit you? You asking a lot of questions about her." He waved me off.

"Nah, it ain't like that. You know I been tryna get at Diamond since back in school."

"Nigga you already fucked her. What more you want?"

"I guess you right. Um, maybe marry her, right?"

I burst out laughing. "Fuck outta here. She'll kill you in your sleep," I said jokingly, but meant every word.

We chilled, talked the shit for a while. Wayne was always a funny nigga. After joke time we end up talking about moves and come ups. That's my favorite conversation. I knew a whole lot about him. One thing was that he always came up with big money plays.

He didn't know that I knew that he was responsible for most of the moves Diamond went on and some she even brung to me. Pillow talk is a bitch. I'ma keep it on the low, right along with the fact that I knew this visit wasn't as random as he playing it off to be.

Just didn't know the reasons for it yet, but I know it'll come to light eventually. Really, I was cool money wise, but a chance to get more is always a plus. I never heard a nigga say I have too much money. Not never. So, I'm not gonna ever say no to a sweet lick so I was all ears as he broke down the play.

He was interrupted by his phone.

"Yeah . . . A'ight . . . on my way."

Click.

He extended his arm to dap me up with plans to meet up. Whoever was on his line had him ready to leave like right now. That was cool with me. Him showing up was slowing me up from getting money anyway.

"Brah, I'ma hit you tomar with more details about the move," he said.

Nigga don't got my number.

"That's a bet, be safe." I saluted him as he turned his car engine over.

He pulled off.

Posted up back to the grind. Not even 5 minutes passed, and I received a text: "I NEED 2 C YOU."

From Diamond.

Curiosity flooded my mind. I didn't text back. I called.

CHAPTER 21

Khalil

This couldn't be true. After searching the house with Naomi, we came up empty. Diamond was officially missing in action. Couldn't understand it.

'WHY WOULD DIAMOND DO SUCH A THING?'

I thought they were tight as butt cheeks. Didn't know there was bad blood. No matter how much I like her I was taught family first and we needed answers.

Had to get out of here. I left the house to try and put my ear to the streets. I knew somebody knew something. Before I left the house I talked to Cortez and he told me he was uptown.

Typical.

All he knew was the hustle. Couldn't blame him though, in this new way of life you have to take care of you and yours.

Thought we were all "family", but I guess that only goes so far. I just tell everybody to look both ways before you cross me. If you cross me I'ma kill you.

All of us were raised in the projects and it gets pretty grimy. Everybody was on their worst behavior. Driving around I was getting madder and madder at the fact of anyone trying to wipe my sister off the map.

Red light.

I inhaled a breath. Usually, I don't even stop for them, but my mind was everywhere, and I needed a second to think. Sat there and maneuvered my mirrors as I thought.

'THEY DON'T REALLY KNOW BOUT KHALIL' I said to myself.

Is this FLYIN'. IS DEEZ NIGGAS TRYN' ME. THEY THINK IT'S SWEET.'

Started thinking about a lot. One thought was that a few niggas around my way did try to collect on that money when we went to the church. The light turned green. I made a left.

The hood was my destination. Living in a world with these cruel, lawless people society done made me a fool and I'm about to become everything they want. I'm sorry mother, but motherfuckers ain't gonna like me. The way this life set up, the grave by twenty-one is oh so likely.

Statistics already told me that I wouldn't live to see the grey on my head but believe me a lot of niggas coming with me. It's too much shit goin' on in the streets. It's a lot of he and she said, but today I'm not tryna hear it. They want beef with me I'ma do them something wrong and empty seventeen bullets straight off in the dome. If it ain't right when questions get asked, it's over for whoever.

Don't know why, but my eyes started to water. Angry tears, I guess. The way I left Naomi in the house played in my head. Emotional. In a ball of tears. The main thought. "Take care of your sister." Pops lasts words.

'I NEED ANSWERS!'

I banged the steering wheel. Livid now. How I felt right then in that moment, anybody could get it. Purposely I drove Naomi's car just so I could draw attention. Wanted smoke. It could be from any and everybody.

Instead of heading up top, I decided to ride down bottom. Knew Cortez was up there hustling and didn't need no pep talk from him right now. All eyes turned as I slowly drove through the streets. I had my window down so everybody could see me. Geeking, waiting for somebody to reach or even blink the wrong way. Had to at least circle the block two or three times.

After hearing what that faggot said about Diamond, I didn't trust nobody around here anymore. Snakes in the grass is how I'll treat them now.

Parked, I sat in the car. I checked my Teflon making sure it was protecting my vital organs. Checked the clips of both Smith & Wesson .40 caliber pistols, then placed them back into my Summit series North face jacket chest pockets and opened my door.

'NEED ANSWERS.'

Seen my first stop. A small crowd of guys was in a huddle. Choose them because when I drove it looked like they were snickering and pointing. Plus, I didn't like the head of the snake in this crew.

It had to be about eight of them. A few of them had blunts of something potent polluting the air. This particular group of niggas was always on bullshit. Not too much info came through the hood without them knowing or having a hand in it. Their eyes and ears stayed in the streets.

"What's up lil nigga? You must be on one. Niggas sayin' you riding around muggin' in shit," Zoe said.

This fake ass nigga's voice and arrogance was already blowing me. He had these niggas shook, but I wasn't a part of that flock. Zoe was a nigga that put in work way before I ever even thought of picking up a gun. His problem was that he still thinks he's the only one willing to squeeze. The smirk he wore only added to my fury.

"Yeah, and . . ." I looked him up and down. "Matter of fact, any of you niggas hear about that bounty that supposed to be on my sister's head?" I said with venom in each word.

Zoe returned my energy and stepped closer. "Don't get it twisted lil' nigga. I'll slap fire out your young ass pulling up on me like that. You need to ask the niggas in y'all circle before stepping to a real nigga." He spit on the ground in front of me.

'THAT WAS CUTE.' I smirked.

I waved him off. "Whatever nigga. Personally, I think your slappers broke 'cause you ain't slappin' shit over here."

I whipped out both .40's one at a time. Zoe didn't flinch, but the rest of them were fidgety. I noticed one nigga tried to make an attempt to reach.

BOOM!

"Uh uh nigga. Let me see y'all hands." The shot went straight through the "helps" forehead, exploding through the back. All hands flew to the sky. "Feeling froggy nigga," I said to another, training the pistol on him. "Then leap!"

I turned my attention back to Zoe who wore a grim expression. I didn't like the comment he made talking about asking my own circle. I asked him again. "What you mean ask my folks? Just tell me so I could get the fuck from around here and handle my business."

"Fuck you and your sister! When I die put my money in the grave." He spit, but this time on me.

I wiped it off and shrugged. "Okay Drake, I'll make sure that get put in your eulogy."

BOOM!

The bullet that splattered his brains silenced him forever. He talked too much, and I been tired of his arrogance. Looking at the rest of his entourage a few of them I fucked with, the rest was somewhat okay.

'DECISIONS. DECISIONS.'

I decided to let them live, but not before I took pictures of Zoe and his flunky. Needed my confirmed kills. As I was backing away, I heard a car coming down the street fast. I trained one gun on the car and the other on Zoe's crew. It was a nice car, and the driver looked familiar. He was familiar. He stopped in front of me, and I lowered the gun from his direction.

"What da' fuck is goin' on?" Cortez asked.

I backed up, walking to his car and opened the door to climb in. My pistol still pointed as I rose the window down to speak to the frightened men. "Hope y'all know it's not personal, but everyone involved is gonna get dealt with accordingly." I raised the window, looking at Cortez. "Pull off."

Adrenaline was rushing. Every time I pulled the trigger of a gun it always did something to me. The constant light squeeze of the handle was close to an orgasm, especially when the bullet found the victim to be a lesser man.

Cortez drove. Where he was headed was unbeknownst to me. I didn't even care. Riding with him I felt safe. Draco on deck, everything you could ever ask for was on demand.

Looking out the window I could feel Cortez' eyes burning a hole through my head. Felt like it was a lot on my plate. The niggas around my way, liars and they fake. I know it's messed up out here, but we all grew up together. What happened to the sandbox code?

With new laws come new mistakes. My peers' mistake was thinking I was that kid that went to the school up the street. He died right along with his parents. Tired of these guys keep tellin' me lies. They wanted the beast, now they got him.

"Khalil!" Cortez called me. I was in a trance. "What was that shit about back there?"

It felt like a dumb question, but before I answer I had to remember he wasn't right there from the start. I inhaled and kept my answer short. "Naomi," and stared at him for a minute before he broke his gaze, pulling off at the green light.

He exhaled the blunt he was smokin' and passed it to me. Looking forward he asked, "What's your plan? Smoke da whole hood?"

"If I have to."

Deep into the ride I remembered that I drove my own car. Things was happening so fast I just forgot. When Cortez pulled up, all I thought was exit plan. "Pull over," I told Cortez.

"Nigga what?! Is you crazy? We on da highway, fool."

"I can't leave my car around there."

"Damn Babyboy, you wait until we get on the highway to start using your brain."

"You ain't gotta take me back. I'll walk, just pull over."

"Shut da fuck up! You sound stupid. I know you going through shit right now, but don't let that be the reason you go out like that. Bullets ain't got no names. You ain't nothing but a confirmed to the next nigga, remember dat."

I waved him off. He the wrong nigga to try and kick some knowledge. He was like the grim reaper. He killed without passion or remorse. "Whatever man. I need the car. It's some shit in there that I need to get," I informed him.

He shook his head and blew a sigh. He knew I wasn't trying to hear that bullshit. Especially not coming from him. His body-count high. he might even be past the limit. He one of them guys that accepted this way of living and didn't plan on going nowhere.

Me and Naomi, we have a plan. As soon as we get enough for the both of us, we outta here. But for now, we have to stay alive and get this bounty squashed.

It started to rain. I hate the rain. It seems like when it rains its death in the air. Most funerals I attended before the Killzone, it always rained. Whenever I found out somebody died, it rained. Now that it's raining, I'm on my way back to Naomi's car. Hopefully, if someone else die, it ain't me.

"What you over there thinkin' 'bout lil bruh?" Cortez asked.

Shook my head. "Nuffin'."

Shit. What wasn't I think about?

It's been so much going on, especially in the last couple of days. My mind was running a mile a minute.

"Yeah, right. Just keep that same temperature when we pull back up. Not really in the mood for a shootout. And what car you drive? You stole one?"

"Naomi's."

"Oh yeah, you definitely on one riding around in that target ship. You need to chill and let the story unfold before you get caught up. We gonna handle it together," he assured me.

I looked at him. He seemed sincere, but I know he had love for both sides. I did too. But one love outweighed the other by miles. Blood thicker than water. I just hope Cortez pick the right side. Me knowing him I think he going to be neutral, but if it comes down to it, I wouldn't hesitate to do what I have to.

Felt like he could read my thoughts. He smirked.

"What's funny?" I asked.

"Nuffin." He shrugged. "You funny lil nigga, dats all."

Pulled up. It seemed like a ghost town, but I wasn't stupid. Niggas always lurkin'. Never would I give these dudes leeway. I just hope they stay cool 'cause they really don't want a wound from the 'K' in the trunk.

Cortez stopped his car in front of Naomi's BMW Coupe. I looked around at every car and window before I exited his car. Gave Cortez dap and he pulled off. I sat in the car and thought to myself.

'I AIN'T GET NOTHING DONE.' I blew a sigh.

Pushed and started the car to life. Music came blasting through the speaker. Silenced it and put the car in drive. Pulling off, I drove to my thoughts.

CHAPTER 22

Naomi

(Few Days Later)

Naomi!! You in here?" I heard Khalil yell from downstairs. I sat in the house watching television. From the looks of things, it couldn't get any worst. Finally talked to Diamond and she seemed normal. Found out she has been with a new boo of hers and that's supposedly the reason why she been missing in action.

Let her believe I was oblivious to her deceit. Definitely didn't believe for a second any of the lies she told over the phone. We supposed to meet up tomorrow, but the way I thinking it has to be a set up. Nothing made sense anymore. Too much has changed in so little time. The only question I have floating in my mind is who told her.

"You deaf, lil ugly?" Khalil asked, bursting in my room.

"Boy, don't you knock?" He shrugged. "What you want?" I asked a little irritated.

"Shit. Just was seeing if you were home. Unlike you, I supposed to have some trim come through. A brotha' got needs." He smirked.

"Ugh, GET OUT!" He laughed and closed my door.

'NASTY SELF.' I shook my head.

I love him though. He really been looking out for me since this bullshit surfaced. I rolled out of bed and put some pants on. I needed to get out of the house. Headed down the stairs. My stomach was growling and doing flips. As I opened the fridge my phone rang. It was an unavailable ID. Still, I answered.

"Yeah?!"

"Hey boo!"

I recognized the voice instantly. "Hey, what's goin' on?" I tried to hide my excitement. It was Cortez.

"Coooolan. You in da crib?"

"Yup."

"I'm 'bout to pull up on you."

I guess he felt that he needed to check on me too. Didn't mind a visit from him. When he arrived, I decided I will tell him about the conversation between me and Diamond.

Inside the fridge was a sad sight. It looked like when Robin Harris dropped off Bebe's kids back home. Wasn't nothing in there but leftover pizza, a box of baking soda and a .99 cent R.C. soda.

Needed to go shopping. Would've asked Khalil, but every time he go, he always bring back snacks and things he like to eat. Everything microwavable. Crazy part was that he knew how to cook, but his patience was long gone. He always stayed on the move. Moving around helped him cope.

Crossed my fingers before I opened the freezer on top of the fridge. Just as I suspected, it was all frozen, instant meals. Really,

I had a taste for a home cooked meal, but since that wasn't possible, I just warmed up some party wings.

In the living room Khalil had his game on pause. Wasn't as interested in video games as he was, but I knew how to play. He was playing Call of Duty. When I un-paused it, I noticed he was online playing with his clan. His character was hidden in a corner. Soon as I stood, I was shot by a sniper.

'OH, IT'S ON!'

I re-paused and was off. The game was intense. These guys were good, more like great. I knew I had to have gotten killed ten times in two minutes. After I got used to their hiding spots, I started killing them.

Didn't even notice how long I was playing until the screen went blue and the CC camera came on. There were two cars pulling up in my driveway. One was Cortez, but the other was foreign.

Cortez' car was in the back of the unknown vehicle. Watching Cortez, he was on point. He got out of his car with gun in hand. The other driver stayed in the car until he approached and opened the door. Khalil came flying down the steps two at a time. He looked my way. "I know you ain't over there fuckin' up my rank."

Waved him off and put the game on pause as I stood up. I took a few steps, headed for the door when Khalil pushed me out of his way, and I fell over the couch. "Move, girl! My trim is here!" he said as I fell on the beanbag couch.

"Dayum, Stink! You press like shit." I rolled over, getting up.

He slid to a stop at the door, looked back at me and brushed his shoulders. "Playa," then opened the door.

The girl jumped in his arms. He caught her as she wrapped her legs around his waist, and they kissed. Cortez slid past, giving Khalil two thumbs up, smiling. I shook my head at their encounter.

I waited until he put the girl down before I said, "Hi, you are?"

Khalil grabbed her hand and pulled her away. "None yuh bizness." She looked back as she was being pulled away.

"Hi, I'm Tammy!" and waved.

I looked over my shoulder to see Cortez on the couch playing the game I paused. I walked over to him and sat. He looked at me, winked, then spoke, "So what's up, boo?"

"Nuffin, sup wit' you?"

"Nuffin, just chillin'."

"Oh, you bruh man from the fif' floor now?" I said, putting up four fingers.

He smirked. "Nah, but uh for real, how you been? Ji, like been worried about you. Diamond told me you hollered at her, so what's up wit' dat? I hope y'all got an understanding and it's squashed."

'SQUASHED!?' I frowned.

She tried to have me killed. How do you just squash something like that? Come to think about it the bounty was still active. Let her tell it she didn't have anything to do with it. "I don't know 'bout that, but we'll see."

"Not what she told me," he said.

"What she say?" I was real interested.

"Nuffin much, but y'all supposed to kick it tomorrow. But me and her supposed to kick it tonight on some ova' shit."

"Is that right?" My heart dropped. Hurt. I didn't want him with her, but I hid it well. I think.

"Yeah, she say she wanna holla at me too 'bout some money moves."

"Where at?" I had to pry and get as much info as I could.

"I dunno. Some joint downtown. It supposed to be a fancy joint. Didn't really care where 'cause she said she would foot da bill. If it's free, it's me."

I smiled. That was his favorite slogan. Especially nowadays when there wasn't too much for free. If this the restaurant I think it is, it's nice. A little jealous he wasn't taking me there, but at least he wasn't taking her. She was taking him. It's a difference.

It was more like a lounge to me though. The atmosphere of it, plus it was pricey. Diamond's little 'THOT' ass was trying her best to move in on Cortez. Crazy part is she only does it out of spite. Little did she know I'm not that pushover I used to be. I have a plan forming in my head and it's coming together.

"Did you hear me, Shawty?" Cortez asked.

"What did you say?"

"I said I think it's that new joint down southwest."

"Um, sounds like a date to me," I said with a little too much emotion I didn't mean to let out.

"Awwww, you wanna come? It's definitely not a date. Me and her, but with you it just might be," he said, licking his lip.

"Whatever." I scooted further down the couch.

"Come here, give me a hug." He playfully spread his arms.

Really, I wanted to jump into them, but reality set in and I smacked his hands down as he leaned over. I heard a yelp. More like a sexual moan. Cortez smiled at me. "You heard that, didn't you?" he asked. "Bet I could make you scream louder," and smirked.

As much as I wanted to see if it was true, I declined the gesture with a wave of my hand. "Boy, not never! That's all you think about."

"Not all the time. Maybe most, but it come second to my money." He brushed his shoulders, then looked at me. "So, you mean to tell me that you ain't thinking about it right this minute. Your lil Stink ain't so little no more. he up there crushing dat lil' piece of fine ass. Must be nice, huh."

"Must be."

We decided to play a little of the game to get our minds off the emotional screams of Tammy. We played for about an hour before Khalil and Tammy came down the stairs. Both of them looked exhausted. Cortez had the look of a proud father, smirking as he watched Khalil sit. Tammy gave off the look of innocence like I didn't just hear her erotic climax over and over again, as she curled up under Khalil.

I looked at them both. "Y'all nasty."

Khalil faced me. "It's the circle of life."

"And you Ms. Thing, umm um." I shook my head and balled my face up. "You know these walls thin." She looked embarrassed. "I'm just messin' with you sweetheart." I turned my attention to Cortez. "Ride with me to the store. I have to go get some real food." He smacked his teeth. "But before we leave, go and grab them hot wings out of the microwave."

He stood up. "What you gonna, eat and drive?" he asked, walking toward the kitchen.

"Nope! I'ma eat while you drive."

CHAPTER 23

Cortez

Just dropped Naomi off. She too funny. The whole time we shopped she tried her best to pick my head for information about my night on the town with Diamond. It was supposed to be tonight, but I didn't give her any details, only an assumption of the location. Really, I just told her to wait until her own meeting with her tomorrow.

It was funny the things goin' on. Well, not funny as in laughing, but like . . . I don't even know the words to express it.

'WILD'

That comes to mind.

I stood on the middle of my block just to blow some time. Even brought some work outside so I could have some spending cash in case Diamond decided to be tight with her funds. I love to purp'. Messing with me she might pull up and I'll have five to ten bands on me just because. You know, just flex on these niggas for the fun of it. These peoples not running me out of my own hood. I've been here since the sandbox. They already made the conditions worst. I'm living in the tank with some blood hungry piranhas. Still, I'm on big dawg statistics. These dudes are runners.

Anybody want it I'm sprayin.' Don't got time to do no tusslin.' This the mind frame I put myself into when I post up. Can't trust these dudes from the new days. If I get threatened, simple, make 'em strip like the Uncle Luke days and get everything off them, including their life. Just another confirmed kill to me.

"Sup' big boy?" Mike asked.

He a cool nigga from around my way that been here since before the bullshit. He 100.

"Tryna smoke?" he asked.

"Uh, yeah. I can't be sober for too long. You know, I gotta stay high," I said, giving him dap.

"Don't even trip. I keep me some fire. Don't you sleep on Ms. Lady, her pussy is torch." He advertised his weed like a woman.

"Whatever nigga! Fly in."

"I'm tellin' you bro, don't be diggin' in her back while you grippin' them thighs, homes. I'm tellin' you. She gonna back back. This ain't no regular pack."

"Nigga! Is you gonna fly in or keep savin' da hoe?"

"You right, you right."

We smoked and reminisced on old times and one story came up that had us laughing hard. He had a broad with him and it made him get animated as I told the story:

"It was about five years ago, before the Killzone. We was broke as a crack fein at the end of the month. He had this fool-proof plan . . . I mean like where should I even start. I guess the beginning," I said to the girl . . .

"Okay so we sat in the trap as the old heads made play after play. We watched so much money exchange that we wanted it for ourselves. I remember getting bored, so I wandered down the hall to the back room and found a pump-action rifle. It was long and heavy—"

"Get to the good part, bruh," Mike interrupted.

"Chill, moe! Let me tell the story." I looked back at the girl, never asked her name. "So, listen. Mike geekin' ass followed me and seen the gun I held. This fool grabbed it and put it in his pants. You should have seen him walking with it. He had a vicious limp as we left the trap, heading to my house. My folks don't ever be home, so it was cool. It was kinda late as the sun disappeared from the sky. In the house, out of the blue Mike say, 'Let's go on a caper.' I didn't mind. We had the gun and no funds so why not, right? She shrugged like, whatever. So, Mike tells me he had a uuv parked around the corner. 'You know what, that is right?'

She nodded yeah and said, "A stolen car, right?"

"Right. Plan was wild, but I agreed—"

"Bruh! The plan wasn't wild, it was a master plan."

"Homes, let me finish." He waved me off and I continued.

The girl started laughing at us feuding.

"So, like I was sayin', the plan was WILD, and I had the wildest part. This fool had us in matching trench coats. Don't know why my folks had these in their closet, but it was the kind that the old school detectives wore; belt, buckle and all. Had us looking like Inspector Gadget, but whatever. I sat in the car for five minutes before I see him running around the corner. He jumped in the car and said, 'Your turn.' He was out of breath as he took his trench off, tossing it in the backseat—'

"Your turn? What did he mean by that? Why y'all didn't go together?" she asked. Mike smiled.

"This is where the story gets interesting." I began, "So, I get out of the car and run down the middle of the damn street toward an approaching squad car, waving my hand hysterically screaming 'help!' My coat was wide open as I ran. The officer jumps out, pointing their gun telling me to raise my hands—"

"What you do?" She was interested.

"What you think?" I screamed. 'Wait, don't shoot! He took everything!" When they noticed my presence, they lowered their weapons. I was ass-naked with socks and shoes on. I pointed, 'he went that way!' in the opposite direction and gave a random description." I finished.

We laughed. Mike wasn't lying about the strand of weed he had. I was in the clouds. There was a moment of silence before the girl broke it with a puzzled face. "So, what they do with you?"

I looked at her and shook my head. "Them pigs got in their squad car and left me on the curb. They didn't treat me like the white people and offer me a ride. They shit was gone."

We smoked the rest of the blunt and Mike rolled out, along with the girl. I was cool. he left me feeling good and in a zone. Still had a few hours before I was to meet up with Diamond. I stayed around the way for about another hour before I decided to get in the car and mash the gas. Tonight, was the night that I figure out what's in Diamond's head and check her temperature.

CHAPTER 24

Diamond

Feel like I'm at a crossroads. Tonight's plan was to figure out what side Cortez was on. Tomorrow, when I meet up with Naomi, I'm just going to kill her myself. It's been a long time coming. Should've been done it. Her spoiled ass has to go.

Khalil will just have to be a casualty of war. Plus, that dream I had felt too real, and I believe Khalil might actually do everything in that nightmare, especially when Diamond was off the map. Revenge brings the worst out of people, but nothing tops envy and I'm very envious of her.

The part that gets me so mad is she acts like she was oblivious to my malice. Ain't no friends in this new world order. All they do is hold you back. Bitch didn't even know I stayed here to help her get out and get my man, but she was too uppity to do the things required. She thinks she is better than me. Maybe she is in the real world, but in this Killzone, I reign supreme. She not built to last.

Had to push thoughts of Naomi to the back of my mind. Tonight, was date night. I was going to treat Cortez to a nice dinner with music, so I could see where his head was at. Hopefully, when it's all over I'll have a partner in crime, and we could blow this city or just take it over.

Either one cool with me as long as he by my side. I would give him the world. He definitely worth it.

"What's taking you so long in that bathroom?" a voice asked.

I looked at the closed door and rolled my eyes. "Hold on, Ma! I'll be finished in a minute."

My mother came to visit. Lucky her, she could come and go as she pleases. Even though she paid to leave, she can always enter and kill for pleasure, but the downside was that she could also get killed. Knowing this fact, she always drove straight here with no stops. The house we were in was hers. Usually I don't come here 'cause I usually be at Naomi's house all the time, but circumstances changed, and I was here now.

In all actuality this what brung my mother here. Her alarm went off and an alert was sent to her phone that I forgot she receives. If it wasn't for my music, I would've heard her when she entered. She walked all the way up on me in my room. If she was somebody else, I would've been a goner. Couldn't nobody else ever get me like that though. Our alarm system is top of the line.

It's not on Naomi's level, but close to it. I needed to invest the one she has, just never had the time.

"Hurry up little girl!" my mother pressed.

I looked in the mirror one final time before opening the door. "Dang Ma! You ain't gotta rush me like that. It's other bathrooms in this house," I said, passing her walking down the hall.

She looked me up and down as I passed. "Thank you for letting me use 'MY' bathroom."

I didn't even look back, just walked to my room to continue getting dressed. My mother could be a real bitch. I guess the apple didn't fall too far from the tree. She didn't know how I really felt about Naomi, no one really knew. I always felt like she thought she was better, but one thing my mother did teach me was that we're all equally fucked up.

This day and age I don't even think she would care if I was to tell her my true feelings, my mother. When the bill passed, she killed her boss and two of her cousins in the same day. I just didn't want her to worry, or worst, try to get involved. She knew I could hold my own, but really when she came, I know she was hopeful for an intruder. She only came to get a few confirmed kills of her own, but she'll never admit it though. It's sweet money.

On the other side of the bridge, she was law enforcement. On this side, not so much.

Date night.

I looked in the mirror. Bad bitch couldn't nobody tell me anything different. Tonight's outfit was definitely going to turn the tide in my direction. Only a homosexual would look the other way. I came down the stairs, a vixen is what I felt like in my strapless shirt with thigh high wrap around heels.

I headed for the door and screamed up the stairs to my mother my farewell. She said something, but I couldn't hear her 'cause the sound of me closing the door silenced her.

In the car I played my R&B shuffle mix. Had to get in a good sexual mood on my way to pick up Cortez. Every love song you could think of played on the way.

When I arrived, didn't even get out of the car. He looked good as he always did. He had me pick him up at his "new" house. It was nice from the outside. He told me that he moved in since the last tenant was gone and the property was vacant and fully furnished. He thought I didn't know the back story, but the streets talk. Cortez's crazy. The man actually just moved himself into somebody else's residence like it was regular. Well, I guess nowadays it is.

"What you smiling at?" he asked, sitting down turning my music off.

"You."

"What I do?" he asked, pluggin' his phone up, shuffling through his own music.

"What didn't you do?" I smiled.

He shrugged. "I guess I am pretty awesome, huh?" He looked me in the eyes, smiling.

"Boy, bye. You too much." I pulled off.

The conversation was natural as the music played softly in the background. 'SO FAR SO GOOD' I thought. Naomi never came up in our conversation. Desperately I wanted to ask but didn't want to ruin the vibe.

Cortez smiled when we pulled up. "I had a feeling you were goin' to bring me here."

I turned to face him. "How you figure that?" I really wanted to know.

"Cause I knew you wouldn't take me to no bullshit ass spot. You know who I am. I'm him." He licked his lips. Damn. I inhaled a breath and bit my bottom lip. he looked like he was leaning in, so I leaned in too. His lips, I wanted a taste.

But no, the nigga was leaning in to grab his phone off the Aux cord. We made eye contact so I played it off.

"Boy move! I'm tryna get in my glove compartment."

He smirked. "Oh, that's what you were doing, huh."

Me and Cortez had only been dealing with each other on this level for a short while, just long enough for us to be confident in our feelings for one another. Even in public I could barely keep my hands off him.

Cortez delighted in teasing me when I was unable to take advantage of his slim, muscular and inviting figure. It became a game between us, and he took every opportunity to drive me crazy with subtle touches and playful innuendos.

It was Saturday night, and we were enjoying a nice dinner at one of them brewhouse restaurants that offered good drinks and loud music, along with a meal. While we sat and enjoyed each other's company, Cortez slipped his hand under the table and began rotating his finger in circles on top of my panties over my clit.

For a good hour he smiled that playful smile while enjoying my moist, but frustrated arousal. He was driving me crazy with lust and all I could think about was getting him home and giving him the hard sex, he so clearly wanted. It was then that Cortez pulled me too close and said, "Did you see the way the waitress was smiling at us?" He whispered in my ear, "She knows I'm playin' wit your pussy. I bet it made her almost as wet as you are."

I bit my bottom lip. "I can't wait to feel you inside me." I slightly moaned.

My heart pounded and my self-control just snapped. After a quick orgasm, I kissed him hard. He almost, well damn near, yanked me out of the booth. Dropping a handful of twenties on the table, he fixed his lustful gaze on me.

"You aren't going to have to wait," he said as he quickly led me outside. I actually yelped with surprise as he pushed me into the backseat of my car.

"What are you doing, Tez?! There are people around! We can't do it here!"

"Sure, we can. It's dark and no one is gonna care anyway. Besides, you've been a bad girl and I'm not waiting until we get home!"

"Oh God! Cortez, I can't believe you're doing this to me." I fake cried like a damsel in distress. I acted like I was saying no as he closed the door and slid over me and I accepted his hot kiss without complaint.

We fumbled hurriedly with our clothes until my skirt was bunched up at my waist and his pants were at his knees. When he brought his throbbing erection up to my soaking wetness my eyes grew wide and my breathing became ragged, and then I took his piece and guided it into me. Him feeling my wetness, he thrust hard, sinking his piece deep into me. I clamped my eyes shut and whimpered in surrender as he began doing me in the backseat.

His hands gripped my shoulders tightly as we found our rhythm and soon, we were in deep as we sexed. I could tell he'd already been on the edge of erupting as I climaxed twice. It only took a few minutes before I felt another orgasm build in my belly.

He flipped me. I held him close and hooked my legs around him as he plunged hard into me. "Come on Tez, do me! Do me hard, baby! I want to feel you inside me!" I moaned.

Moments later his body became hard as steel and he drove his piece deep as it could go and exploded into me. It was an incredible moment until I looked through the slightly fogged window.

I seen a figure approaching. I knew there wasn't a creep watching us. It was coming through the parked cars, hunched over, swiftly making their way to us. Cortez looked. His face didn't even seem surprised as I too noticed who it was.

"Naomi!?" I reached in the back pocket pouch of the passenger seat and grabbed my .40 caliber pistol. "Nigga you tried to set me up! And for her at that!!"

The backseat of my car looked like a lightshow as I pumped seven holes into Cortez' body. I opened the backseat and pushed him out onto the pavement.

Shots! Multiple of them hit the car as I crawled to the other side getting out. I ducked and returned fire to a blind target recklessly.

The shooting lasted all but ten seconds, then an eerie silence. "Naomi!!" I yelled. "So, this what it is, huh?"

"Bitch, you already know! YOU DID THIS TO US!"

I looked at my empty gun. Didn't know what she had so I had to try something. "Look, I know you mad, but this ain't what you want. This ain't you. You made me kill my future husband. Now you gonna make me kill you." I tried to peek and see if I could find her position but couldn't. "SAY SOMETHING!!" I yelled but received nothing but crickets. After two minutes I stood to look around. She was gone.

CHAPTER 25

Khalil

The phone in my pocket rang consistently. I ignored it a few times, but the caller was persistent. As soon as I reached to answer, the line went dead. It was Naomi.

Was about to call her back when a chilling text came through. 'CORTEZ DEAD.' The message made me frown. I was just with him earlier in the day. He told me he was meeting up with Di-amond. Wanted to go with him, but if he would have agreed I probably would've smoked her sexy ass on sight. Inside I was mad as shit she nerver let me do that to her. Would've dawged' that box.

I unlocked my screen to call Naomi back. Needed to hear this revelation out of her mouth.

"H-Hello." I could tell she was crying.

"S-Stink, she killed him. It was all my fault."

"Who killed who? Slow down."

The crying started to become heavy. It had me tight. Always hated to hear my sister cry.

She sniffed snot. "Diamond! She killed Cortez."

There it was. Stamped. I was at a loss for words for a second as it silenced me.

"Hello?"

"I'm here, sis. Where you at?"

"Home."

"What happened?"

Naomi told me the story of how it happened. All I could do was shake my head, mourning my big homie. After she finished, I ended the call telling her I was on my way there. Diamond is a cold-hearted bitch. From what Naomi told me she didn't even hesitate when she filled my man up with lead.

It had to be on sight when I finally ran into her. I stood up out of the bed quickly putting clothes on. I had promised Courtney my time since I haven't seen her since the last move, she put me up on. But duty calls and I had to get up out of there.

Still was trying to wrap my head around what Naomi just told me. 'Cortez dead!?' Courtney had a frown on her face. She always looked sexy to me when she pouts. Good thing was that she didn't argue. She heard the conversation and knew there wasn't any talking me out of leaving.

Cortez always the one telling me not to give these niggas lead way. He knew Diamond was a cold-blooded killer first, everything else came after. Nowadays you have to take heed to what the streets say. Diamond played with my sister and Naomi didn't even deserve it.

I hope Diamond knew that I wasn't gonna never quit messing with my family. Full speed is how I'm coming. This whole situation had me out of my element, but it was definitely going to get handled.

Finally had my clothes on and was about to leave when Court-ney ran up on me in a pair of boy shorts and nothing else. "Need me to come with you?"

Thought about it for a second. "Nah, I'm good. I'll see you later tonight."

"You coming back?"

'NOPE.'

"Maybe tomar'. It depends on my night," I said, closing the door.

If I would've stayed, I knew she would have convinced me to let her tag along, especially lookin' how she was lookin'. Courtney buss her gun too, but she ain't no Diamond and I didn't want her blood on my hands.

In the car I pulled my vest over my head and started the igni-tion to the Coupe. Might as well say it's my car now 'cause Naomi haven't drove it since that flyer started to circulate. But me, I be geeking for some smoke from anybody.

Checked my clip on my extended nine-millimeter and put it back in the butt of the gun, cocking it back and placing one in the chamber. Satisfied, I placed the gun on my lap as I pulled out of the driveway.

The sky was black, the moon was bright, but not a star in the sky. Neon lights illuminated the street as I drove. Cruising through the city I popped the cork of the bottle of Remy 1738 that Cortez left in the backseat and took a sip. I lifted the bottle in the air slightly. "Here's to the ones that I got." I sipped. "And cheers to the wish you were here, but you're not," and drank more.

Felt the burn in my throat as my eyes watered. Memories flooded my mind. Guess everybody hurt some days. These times it's most days. There's a time where I remember when I didn't know any pain, even believed in forever and thing would stay the same.

Now, my heart feels like January when I think about how much has changed. You can feel it in the streets; gun shots and distant screams. Driving, a memory came to mind . . .

"Why you walking like that?" I asked Cortez."

"The F&N make my hip limp, regular shit."

Shook my head at his joke. He always had a wild rebuttal when questioned. It was his nature. We was in the neighborhood, this was before the laws changed. I wasn't even in the streets, but he was. Naomi always told me stay away from him. In her word, 'He bad news.' I hated being told what to do, so every chance and every time I seen him outside, I was right under his wing.

This was my first move with him. Well, first period. There I stood, short, little dude, but my pistol tall. Interior of me scared to death, exterior bluffin' good. Felt like Cortez carried the key to the city. His name carried weight. His favorite line, 'DON'T FUCK WIT DUDES, MOST OF EM FAKE.' He was a product of the city, straight from the gutter and to lose him still didn't really register.

"You ready lil' nigga?" he asked.

"Yeah, no question."

Really, I wasn't, but it sounded convincing. Learned the hard way the streets definitely don't show no love when pockets are hurting, and his was. I stayed broke so this was going to put whatever in my pocket.

He stood on the side of the door, not visible. "Well, knock on the door, nigga."

I gave two knocks, not too aggressive, but loud enough to be heard. Could have sworn Cortez heard my heart pounding inside my chest as I waited for the door to open.

"Fuck is you!?" A guy opened the door.

"Uh-uh—" I started to stutter. The words just wouldn't come out.

Cortez bent the corner making himself visible, hitting the guy with the butt of his assault rifle. "Shut up, nigga! Nigga always talking like a gangsta, running your mouth." The guy fell into the house as he approached. "Lil I run in the house." He ran up on dude, putting the gun in his mouth. "Talk shit now!"

I came in looking behind me and closed the door. Cortez looked at me. "Pull your gun out, lil nigga!"

I reached into my dip, pulling out this long 4x4 Magnum and scanned the area. Noticed two guys on the couch so I pointed my cannon at them. Cortez gave his attention to the victim after he felt secure that I had him covered.

"Earlier you did all that loud talkin' knowing you didn't really want this problem. I told you I knew where your family lived. Now that I'm here, hope you know the verdict."

"Come on homie, you ain't even gotta do this. I apologize. This shit ain't for us. You can have all this shit. It's a safe in the kitchen. Combo is 8-14-4." I could hear the fear all in the guy's voice.

"Thanks. I could have it?" The guy nodded. "Cool, but still, I ain't 'bout to spell it out homie. You shouldn't have did what you did."

A single round went through his head, silencing anymore of his pleads that was sure to come. Cortez looked at me. "Kill them too!"

Still, to this day I never knew what dude did to deserve getting left in his living room like that. I smiled, remembering my first body. That was a minute ago. Finally pulled up to the crib. Naomi was on the porch, looking like G.I. Jane, fatigues and all.

She was ready. I noticed dried tears and sweat. The only thing missing was blood. It's nothing left in the city for us. We were close to our money goal, so after this Diamond situation we could hopefully roll out.

Naomi stood up. "This bitch have the nerve to tell me to meet up with her, still."

"Let's kick it, den." I was geeking.

Diamond was doing the most, but nigga like me I be sayin' the least. I'm tryna go, no rap. They done fucked up by giving me the right to bear arms, but now with that bounty, I have to do so carefully 'cause we are the ones they plot on. That didn't stop nothing though. We gonna keep it rollin' like the camera on us or them peoples on us. Like the slogan say, 'BORN TO LOSE BUITT TO LAST.' I'm built to last. I needs mine. Fuck all the extra.

CHAPTER 26

Naomi

This bitch have the nerve to tell me to meet up with her!" I told Khalil as he approached. The audacity of this broad had him livid. These bitches don't even know what loyalty like. But it's cool. I got everything she need and it's on the way.

"Let's go!" Khalil said. He looked emotional himself. I knew we couldn't go anywhere in this condition.

"Not yet, Stink. Come with me to the backyard for a minute."

Had to think. I will not be disrespected, and damn sure wasn't gonna get played or bitched. Diamond dropped the ball when she showed her cards. It's crazy to me still. Was with her right or wrong. Didn't believe in switching, but I see clearly now that she changed the rules.

"Here, fire this up." I tossed Khalil a pouch of weed. He looked at me crazy. He knew I didn't smoke enough to have this much.

"Where this come from?" He grabbed it, examining it like it was fake or not to his standards.

"It was Cortez's. He left it the other day."

As the potent strand entered my lungs almost instantly, I started to feel like summer. The skies turned bright blue even though it was night. The lighting bugs looked like close stars. Was even tempted to make a wish. Felt myself smiling as I stared at the sandwich bag of tree. My mind was playing tricks. It reminded me of honey; sticky but made things sweet. Maybe it was ice cream, creamy and made my crotch moist. I bit my bottom and closed my eyes.

"What the hell you doing?" Khalil asked with a screw face.

"Nothing!" I quickly answered, getting myself together.

"Bull-shit. You over there sucking on your bottom lip like you enjoying a meal. You hungry? Got da munchies?" He giggled and reached for the blunt. I pulled it away, declining.

I did feel good. Could see why people smoke as much as they do. Definitely had me feeling good. All I wanted to do was go to a pretty place where the flowers grow. This was nothing like when I was in the third grade sniffing glue, wired up, completing the rubix cube in minutes. "Feel like we just met, but I think I'm in love with you," I said, looking at the blunt.

Looking at Khalil as he tried to snatch it yet again, he was on it too, so it's safe to say he loves it too. "Stink, I'm the highest in the room."

He laughed uncontrollably at me as I finally passed him the blunt. Crazy. That's all I remember . . .

"Stink!!" I screamed when I woke up. I felt upside down and discombobulated. Looked around and noticed I was in my bed with last night's attire still on. The sun shined bright through the window, making me squint. Had to adjust to the rays as Khalil entered my room with a blunt dangling from his lips. We made eye contact. "What you give me last night?!"

"Shit, you gave it to yourself." He blew smoke.

"Is that it?" I nodded with my head pointing.

He pointed to the blunt in his hand. "What, this?"

"Yeah, stupid! Give it here!"

It's amazing. The feeling of the blunt. Guess I was a problem to Diamond, but she would never get a resolve. My pain run deep, the smoke mellow me out. People shooting at me, trying to slay me, but today it ends.

Today, I'm only here to send one message and the bullets going to make her respect it on the way to her next life. It's on sight when I see her, dearly departed will be her final farewell. The Killzone was working in the government's favor. They really didn't want our money, they wanted to take us out. This was going to be the day I help them out.

Khalil was ready, dressed and everything. "What's da' move, you ready or what?"

"We have to make a stop first. Give me a minute."

He nodded, closing my room door. No need for a shower, things were going to get pretty dirty today. Khalil didn't know, but after this move, we're leaving to the other side of the bridge. All I had to do was stop at Cortez' house and collect the money out of his safe. He gave me the combination when he decided that leaving wasn't in his near future. There was way over the amount needed to ghost this city.

It was a time when I used to look into my father's eyes. They were so reassuring. In a happy home, I was the queen and he made sure I had a golden throne. The security he provided had me feeling he'll be here forever and be worry free. Those days were gone, but the memories were on the wall.

As I put my clothes on for war, thoughts of Diamond made tears fall, angry tears. Diamond was a girl of a different kind. We walked the streets and school yard like we ruled the world. Never thought I'll lose her like this.

Young. We were so young. I think of her now but miss the then. Songs constantly remind me of the friend I lost. The only thing that keeps me somewhat stable is the words of my father.

'DON'T WORRY SWEETHEART, ALWAYS REMEMBER HEAVEN HAS A PLAN FOR YOU.' I smiled at the thought.

Walking in a straight line was never Diamond's style and now it made much sense. Thought we had the same heartbeat, but hers is going to fall behind. Damn, she was good. Always talking with a fake smile, never had a clue.

Left my room and headed down the stairs. Family photos lined the wall and Diamond was in many of them. Khalil was in the living room playing his favorite game, Call of Duty. It seemed to always put him in the killing frame of mind.

"Come on, Stink."

He raised a finger. "A'ight, hold up, two minutes."

I walked to the kitchen. On the counter was a bottle of Patron. I drank two shots and accessed my plan. The burning sensation, along with the blunt, put me in the state of mind I needed to be in. Khalil yelled from the living room; he was ready. But before I head to meet Diamond, I had to make a quick pit stop.

In the car we headed to the Gunshop. It was a couple of blocks from my house. Crazy enough, it used to be a Pizza Hut. Now it's named the Gun Hut. Instead of a pizza box as the logo, it was converted into a box of open bullets, slowing spinning high in the sky.

Khalil and I entered the store. Ironically, the owner was a retired marine and he stood proud behind the counter. He was young, but I could tell he was thuggish.

"Welcome," was his greeting. I gave him a nod, walking down the first aisle.

There was guns galore. I mean every aisle. Khalil grabbed two handguns without a second thought. One of the guns had a drum that Khalil called 'dog nuts.' But me, was undecided and thought to ask the owner, "Hey."

"Mmm," he nodded.

"What's your specials for today?" I asked, trying to be funny.

To my surprise, there was really a special going on and he explained them all to me. It wasn't bad, but I didn't really want any assault rifles. Still, I wanted another recommendation from him.

I gave him a scenario of how I was trying to pull up and it put a smile on his face as he responded.

"Right now, just for you, I'm going to give you something to make a nigga beg please. When the bullet fly by, I guarantee you'll feel a slight breeze. In that same second your victim will drop to their knees."

"Let me get it."

CHAPTER 27

Diamond

Here I sat on the middle of the carpet Indian style in a pair of athletic leggings and a bra. My hair was a mess. The dress I wore the night before was rolled in a ball in the corner of the room. My hands still wore the blood of Cortez' deceit. He was gone and Naomi made me do it. Why did she have to try and use him to set me up? Why did he agree? So many questions would go unanswered. So many questions ran laps like a marathon as I cleaned the assault rifle that I plan to introduce to Naomi.

I loved that boy, and she took him away from me. Each .223 shell I placed in the thirty round clips had to have a sentimental meaning which is why I smeared Cortez' blood on each one, so when it penetrates Naomi, she could take some of him with her.

In the background I played some throwback Three 5 Mafia tracks to level my mental. After last night I figured me, and Naomi was on sight as of now. This not a game she wanted to play with me, but now it's on. The music playing had me hype as I listened to the lyrics. Thoughts of the past only angered me. I tossed the rifle on the bed and caught my reflection in the mirror. Looking at myself and analyzing my life, I knew I didn't have nothing left.

Even before the laws changed, I've been blasting my gun and laughing at the results that even my mother thinks my mind was gone. On the real I haven't never crossed a man that didn't deserve it.

Getting treated like anything but royalty was unheard of. Had to make sure that people watched how they talked to me or about me. If they didn't, it was facts that they would be laid in chalk.

I punched the mirror at the person I've become. Shaking my head, thinking of the situation. I can't live a normal life being raised in these conditions. I had to be down with the bad team. Watching all them bullshit shows growing up, shit had me chasing dreams.

Know I'm an educated bitch but with faults. I always have death on my mind. A Mac-11 on the bed right beside the AR-15 I just loaded put a gleam in my eyes. Already know murder ain't nothing but a heartbeat away. That's why I'm living this life, do or die.

Is it power in the money or money in the power? Everybody is running, but half of them not looking at what's goin' on in the kitchen. Even I don't know what's cookin' so I attack head on.

Naomi told me that I was going to learn, but I'll be damned if she going to be the one to teach me. She don't even understand, her methods would never reach me. All I knew was that her life would soon be over, and the luck would run dry.

Leaving my room, the smell of eggs and bacon attacked my nostrils. Moms was still here. Thought she would have been gone by now—her words. Following my nose, I headed down the stairs toward the kitchen where I found much more. Didn't know what got into my mother, but there was a plate with a big ass omelet, bacon, corned beef hash, grits and sausage.

The sight of food made my mouth water as I licked my lips how dogs do when in this same moment. I walked to the plate, about to take a seat and grub, when my mother came around the corner.

"Uh Uh Diamond! You know damn well that's not for you."

I looked at her confused, because it was another plate with the same thing right across from the one, I stood in front of. Before I could ask why, I heard a toilet flush.

"Who in the bathroom?" My eyes shot straight to the hallway.

"My date and that's his plate."

As I looked around, I started to notice all the things I paid no attention to the first time. There was a whole different setup. A rose in the middle of the table, orange juice and slow music softly playing in the living room.

My mother pointed to the stove and told me to fix my own plate. The night before I thought I was dreaming when I heard the passionate sounds of lovemaking switching to rough sex.

"You couldn't make me a plate," I said, walking to the stove. My back was to the entrance of the kitchen when I heard him.

"Hey baby! It smell good up in here."

I stopped dead in my movements, dropping the spatula looking to the ceiling. The voice was too familiar, and I was nervous to turn around. When I did, it was shocking.

"WAYNE!? What da fuck, boy! You fuckin' my mom's?"

"Your mom?!" He looked confused. "I swear I didn't even know; you have to believe—"

My mother cut in. "Yes, he is and what do that have to do with you?" I could see her anger building as she placed her hands on her hips.

'Cause I'm fuckin' him too, mom, is what I wanted to say.

"No reason at all, mom. It's just that we went to school together, that's all."

"Okay and so what? He grown now. Is he off limits or something?"

"No, mom," I said, turning back around fixing my plate.

My mother began setting up a placemat for my plate. I gave Wayne a side eye. He knew what it mean. (DON'T SAY SHIT!) He sat down and started eating. I walked toward the living room with my plate. No way was I going to eat with both of them.

Ain't that some shit. Stella tryna get her groove back. Not even made at her. But Wayne, he got me fucked up. He think I'm stupid if he believe that I think he didn't know who my mother was. He seen her plenty times growing up.

Thoughts of him were side bared. The eggs were good, especially how she put multiple cheeses in the middle and it was melted. Haven't had a breakfast like this since grade school but guess that young dick made her do wonders.

After breakfast I headed back to my room to finish getting myself together. Placing the guns in my bag, I decided to wear the Mac-11 like a purse with a string for shoulder support. Was short on ammo so I needed to grab a few shells. That was nothing to complete.

About to head out when I reached for my doorknob, but it was pulled opened by Wayne. I gritted on him. "Oh, my mother let you come out to play?"

"Don't do that. Didn't even know that was your moms."

"Where she at now?"

"Shower, can we talk?"

I pulled his shirt, bringing him into the room. "Shut up! No talking." Grabbing him I pulled his shirt over his head and started kissing his bare chest.

"What you doing?" he asked, looking toward the hallway.

"I said no talking. She going to be in there for at least twenty minutes. This my dick, now give me some."

His eyes lit bright. I could only imagine what he was thinking. Probably that he was the man, fucking a mother and her daughter.

I pushed him to the bed and jumped on top of him as I unbuttoned his pants. His tool began to rise. Didn't want to suck it cause I'm sure my mother's juices still on him. I know Wayne pretty well. He don't wash until he gets home. He like to keep the sex on him.

I climbed on top of him guiding him inside of me. His thickness was a surprise every time as I moistened, turning the pain into pleasure. Quickly I bounced, trying to catch my orgasm. "Ah SHIT!!" I yelped as I came for the first time.

Wayne placed his hand over my mouth. I smacked it away and he pushed me off of him. I landed on my back and he quickly got up turning me around and placing his hand forcefully in the back of my head and his other hand on my lower back forcing me to arch my ass high in the air.

He plunged into me from the back. The thigh to ass repetitions was rapid as I matched his stroke, throwing it back. I loved the way he makes my body feel. I already knew how my mother felt when she got defensive in my questioning.

He pounded harder and it felt better with each stroke. His legs locked as his warm sensation shot into me. In the same second I heard the shower stop. he jumped off the bed, pulling his pants up. I grinned as I noticed the smirk on his face.

Putting my leggings back on I stroked his ego. "Boo, you know you still mines, right?"

"Already know, but what about your mother?"

"Don't worry about her, boo."

"Nuff said."

YEAH, I BET NIGGA.

"But I need you to ride with me to handle some business."

"Business?!"

"Yeah boo. Big money business too. All you gotta do is watch my back."

"Shid a'ight, when?"

"Right now. I was on my way."

After our conversation my mother walked into the room. She looked at Wayne. I'm about to head across the bridge. I'll call you, okay?" He nodded, walking to her kissing her passionately. I was tight a little bit.

Then my mother looked at me. "I'll be back tomorrow. You need me to bring something back?"

"Nah, I'm good ma. Be safe."

With that she was gone. I looked at Wayne and asked him was he ready. He was. Locking the house down we left. In the driveway I seen a sexy Infiniti Q60s. It was two-tone, black and cranberry. The cranberry was on the bottom. I looked at Wayne suspiciously. "you been making moves, huh?"

"I didn't choose the Coupe life. The Coupe life chose me."

That was cute. "Let me drive." He tossed me the keys and I smiled as I sank into the leather seats. The car still had the new smell. The engine was silent when it turned over. Cruising down the street it was quiet in the car. Guess Wayne grew suspicious. Don't know why. He was safe. "So, where we going?"

"Uptown." I kept my answer short.

Wayne pulled his gun off his hip and opened the glove compartment. Noticing the pistol, I asked to see it. It was real pretty and shiny. Looked new. A GLock 18 with a fifty-clip extension. He smiled giving it to me.

"You like?"

I grabbed it. "Sure do." Then I up'd it to his face.

"W-wait!!"

He put his hands up but was too late as I held the trigger of the fully automatic trigger. His body only stopped shaking after I released the trigger. I looked over at his bullet riddled body and shook my head.

"I know you didn't think I was gonna let you get that shady shit off. At least I gave you one last fuck."

Driving, I enjoyed a fat blunt that Wayne was about to spark. I looked at his corpse and nodded. The blunt was good. After a few pulls I put it out. Didn't want to get too high. I become paranoid and that wasn't an option today.

Naomi never called me back, but how she felt I'm sure she'll definitely hit me back. I pulled into a strip mall that held a few stores. Parking, I pulled into a spot. I had to run into one of the stores to grab some items for today's task, just a few failsafes. I giggled to myself thinking of Wayne as I entered the store. 'That fool thought I was going to let that shit ride.' Naomi next . . .

CHAPTER 28

On sight. The meaning of the phrase is deadly. Whenever you see your enemy that's where it's supposed to go down. The moment of truth.

The sun was a scorching ninety degrees, not common for the month of September as a few light sprinkles of rain came and went. A rainbow shot across the sky giving the illusion of a beautiful day. Beautiful days didn't exist anymore in the City of Corruption. It's a dog-eat-dog way of living.

Diamond was in the Dollar Tree buying a few items that she needed to tie up a few loose ends. She was oblivious to the fact that Naomi and Khalil was two stores down buying the ammunition for her demise.

Fate. Some would say that they were in the same strip mall for that reason. Destiny is one in the same. Someone was going under and there would be no coming back. This was all or nothing. The feeling was driving them crazy. This day will bleed before the night falls. Couldn't nobody let their guard down. If one does, the other would pull the rug.

Khalil exited the store first. Naomi right on his heels as they both looked around scanning the area. Khalil gave a head nod towards the parking lot.

"Ain't that the dude Wayne's car?"

"Who?"

"I seen him with Cortez a few times. He probably don't even know about Cordy yet. I wonder what store he in."

Naomi shrugged. "I dunno."

"Duh, it wasn't a literal question. I could recognize that car anywhere. That paint job is like dat," Khalil said, walking closer to the car to get a better look. As he looked inside the car, he noticed Wayne in the passenger seat, dead. "Oh shit! Somebody punished his ass."

Naomi didn't even look in the car. She turned to the row of stores. "Stink, duck!" Rapid fire came flying her way as she hid behind a parked car. Bullets tattooed the opposite side of the vehicle as she reached for her weapon. "Khalil! It's Diamond!" she said, finally looking at her brother. Her eyes bubbled. "STINK! No, no, no." She turned Khalil over to see his upper torso leaking through his white tee. "You better not do this to me, Stink." Tears wailing in her eyes.

Khalil was going in and out of consciousness as the AR-15 bullets continued to thunder. There was a pause.

"She empty, hold on Stink."

Naomi stood, took aim and fired. Diamond ran for cover as she tried to reload the assault rifle. She flipped the clip entering a fresh thirty rounds of .223 shells.

A shot pierced Diamond's shoulder that spent her around and dropped her to the pavement. Naomi seen an opportunity. She looked at Khalil who wasn't moving. She decided to run up on Diamond.

There was a woman with her child in the line of fire crouched behind a car. Diamond ran toward them and grabbed the mother as a shield. Trying to protect his mother, the little boy grabbed at her arms. Diamond pushed the little boy away and put two shots in his chest that sent the child soaring in the air then landing with a thud.

The mother was hysterical as Diamond held her as a shield, firing rounds at a running Naomi. Naomi seen the little boy fly back after the bullets struck him. He looked like a ragged doll as he rolled. She ducked for cover.

Naomi had a decision. The "Killzone" version of herself wanted to shoot through the human shield to get at Diamond; the other version of her before this bill was passed was indecisive.

Khalil was a few cars back. Naomi looked in his direction as she kneeled. "STINK! . . . SAY SOMETHING!!"

Silence.

There weren't any responses. That only angered her as she took a deep breath and stood up firing her weapon. Three shots entered the human shield as two .223's tagged Naomi. A loud scream of pain let her as she fell to the pavement, instantly dropping her gun.

Diamond tossed the lady and began slowly approaching Naomi.

"See, Nay, you never let me shine like the diamond I am." She took a knee when she reached Naomi and brushed her hair out of her face. "I always said I'd catch you when you fall . . . GET UP BITCH! Tell me how it feels, huh. You sitting up there, feeling so high and mighty! You know I'm the one that put you up there. Now it's time for you to why the sky will always be lonely." Diamond stood straight up and pointed the Mac-11. "Bye Nay-Nay, time to join your brother and your parents.

BOOM!

An explosive shot knocked off portions of Diamond's head as she dropped the submachine gun and fell face first. Khalil stood behind her holding his abdomen, barely able to stand up straight. He looked to the sky breathing short breaths.

"I-I told you I got her . . . Pops." Then collapsed.

Noami slowly stood up. Her vision was blurred. It started to drizzle slightly as she watched the rain wash blood down the parking lot into the drain. Diamond was dead. Her mission complete.

Naomi stepped over Diamond's corpse and stood in front of Khalil. Grabbing him up with little to no help from Khalil, she managed to put him in the passenger seat. Getting back in the car she pulled off.

As she drove, her eyes kept wandering off to check on Khalil. She spoke and his responses were one-word responses. He needed medical attention and needed it urgently.

Naomi tried to keep her composure, but the weight of her reality was heavy. In her life she seen so much blood and it changes you. She drove straight to Interstate 495 headed for the Virginia border crossing. In the trunk was a load of money, their ticket out of the Killzone.

It was finally over.

The whole drive across the bridge Naomi talked to Khalil about their new beginnings. She rambled. She laughed, cried, and joked the whole way in happy tears.

Finally, it was time to get Naomi pulled to the barricade and was met by heavily armed soldiers.

One of them approached. No non-sense in his voice. "Your Card?"

"I-I don't have one, b-but the money to purchase two is in the trunk," she stammered.

He looked into the car and replied. "That'll cost you one hundred and fifty thousand or your confirmed kill rate receipt."

I looked at him with confusion. "No, Naomi need two cards. Y'know, for me and my brother."

He looked over at Khalil. "He's dead, ma'am."

CHAPTER 29

Beeeep...Beeep...Beep
The monitor in the makeshift clinic kept a steady ping with the heartrate. Naomi's condition was fairly well compared to a couple of days ago. The killzone had almost gotten the best of her and claimed her life. Her eyes flickered. Looking at the back of her eyelids for a while caused a glare as her vision began to focus.

"Where, where am I?" Naomi was discombobulated and confused. Didn't anything make sense. Nothing looked familiar as she glanced around.

There was a silhouette in the corner of the room that jumped at the sound of Naomi's voice. "Oh my!" The elderly lady stood and headed toward the door yelling, "She's awake! She's awake!"

Naomi tried to lift her body but she was still very weak. She couldn't wrap her mind around what was going on? Who was the old lady? And who was she calling too? All Naomi knew was that she wasn't going to be laid up in some strangers make-shift clinic when they arrived. She looked around for any type of weapon she could use to defend herself.

Pulling the IV out her arm, Naomi now had a thin pole that she planned to use like a spear for anyone that came through the door. She stood and took position on the side of the wall, opposite of the door. When the door opened she would be perfectly hidden behind it.

Naomi arranged the bed giving it the illusion that she was still tucked comfortably under the sheets. Chatter could be heard as the voices neared. The door opened and Naomi cocked her arm back ready to swing for the fence at whoever's head. "Naomi? Sweetie are you awake?" The voice was calm and familiar. Most important it wasn't a threat.

Naomi lowered the pole and let it drop upon recognition of the man. "Ol' Man, Harry!?"

"Hey Sweetheart! What you doing out of bed?" He tried to usher her back.

Ol' man Harry was the neighborhood security guard in her community. He held guard at the only entrance and exit of the neighborhood. Friends of the family before the laws changed. Genuinely he was concerned.

As Naomi walked back to the bed another voice stopped her mid-stride, "Nay Nay! Sup' sleepy head? How are you feeling?" It was Khalil.

'Khalil?! My Stink?'

"H-How? W-what happened? You were dead in the passenger seat when we made it to the checkpoint."

"What the hell you talkin' about, Nay?" Khalil turned toward Harry, "Aye Ol' Man, what you put in that drip bag over there? She talking 'bout some checkpoint. That money gone!"

"Gone? What you mean gone? I mean, like what happened? How are you here? And why aren't you in a bed beside me since you aren't dead?" Naomi sent questions rapidly. She was so confused. Her body ached and she wondered why?

"Dead? Why the hell would I be dead? I'm the fuckin' Hitman! I cant die. Your ass should be the one that's dead. you was shot with a frickin' AR-15 that almost knocked your shoulder off along with your head."

"W-What? You was the one that got shot, and multiple times at that by that big army gun, not me!"

"Yeah okay, says the one in the bed with bandages on her wrapped in granny's good shawl," He clowned, "But since you seem to have amnesia I'll recap the evenings events for you...

***

TWO WEEKS AGO

Naomi and Khalil were in the store buying ammo for their upcoming meeting with Diamond. After getting enough ammo to kill Diamond and a small community they exited the store. Across the way Khalil noticed a car. "Aint that the dude car, Wayne's car?"

"Who?"

" I saw him Cortez a few times. he probably don't even know about Cordy yet. I wonder what store he in."

Naomi shrugged, "I dunno."

Khalil gave her a look then advanced toward the car. he was positive of the owner. No one had a car like Wayne and the paint job was immaculate. he looked inside the car and noticed Wayne in the passenger seat, "Oh shit! Somebody punished his ass! Looks like he wont be needing this ride anymore." He reached to grab the keys that dangled out of the ignition.

Retrieving the keys with a smile on his face he stood up in the nick of time to notice Diamond turning her assault rifle in their direction. With bubbled eyes he screamed, "NAY DUCK!"

Semi-automatic spurts from the AR-15 made Naomi's body turn a 720 before hitting the ground. Khalil ducked behind the car and pulled Naomi from the sight of fire as bullets riddled his new ride. He covered his ears with both hand cannons as if they were earmuffs. Khalil glanced at Naomi who had bubble eyes as she coughed blood holding her abdomen. "Hol' on, Nay! Don't you bitch up and die on me!"

Diamond stopped firing in order to reload her clip. The second it took to do it was all Khalil needed to stand up and let off a few rounds of his own as he progressed toward Diamond.

The strip mall parking lot was half occupied with a few vehicles spaced out for cover. Diamond took full advantage and hid behind a truck that sat idle. Looking inside the vehicle she noticed it had keys in it and the driver ran to the closest store as a haven from the gun battle.

Diamond jumped in the driver seat and turned the ignition. the truck was already smoking from the multiple rounds that attacked its frame but it still started up. Joy ran through her veins as she put the truck in gear and pulled off for her great escape...

"Wait! Are you telling me that back stabbing bitch got away!" Naomi asked through clenched teeth. She started to hyperventilate thinking of the worst. The food gates of her emotions became visible and Khalil couldn't take it.

"Okay, okay, no she didn't get away. She is in the other room and wants to talk. She says she's sorry and want to be friends. I believe her." Khalil informed.

"Sorry! Friends? Has she lost her damn mind!" Naomi made an attempt at getting up again but Ol' Man Harry rushed to her side.

"Khalil, stop that lying to your sister. You're making her vitals jump everywhere. Now tell her the truth,y 'hear." Harry rubbed Naomi's back as she stared daggers into Khalil.

"Yea, Stink! What really happened?"

"Okay, okay," He raised both hands in surrender, "So while you was on the ground trying to paint the street red, I was putting in that work. Diamond did actually try to pull off in the truck but I guess she thought I was still shooting from behind the car beside you when really I was advancing with each shot. You know how i do. GTA Style. I had my armor and endless bullets, wasn't no hiding.

"so by the time she turned the ignition to put the truck in gear I was at the window putting holes in that pretty weave she had. I left her ass right in the drivers seat." He finished.

"And our money to leave?"

"Gone."

"What you mean gone?"

"Well, not all of it but most of it. During our gun battle with Diamond a few other guys tried to collect on our I guess. Maybe they didn't know and just tried to get an easy confirmed kill but whatever the case may had been, after I got you into the car, I headed here to see Ol' Man Harry and she directed me to his wife who patched you up.

"But we were chased and another gun fight erupted. shit was crazy! They had that shit too! But luckily they weren't accurate like me. By the time they finished shooting our car was engulfed in flames and a minute later it exploded. It was raining cash! Shit had me tight.

"I killed a couple of them but the other two got a way and I didn't bother to chase them. i did have you on the curb bleeding out in shit. So I stole another car and hauled ass to our house where Ol' Man Harry was at the gate and brought you here."

"So how much money do we have, stink?" Naomi asked in an exhausted breath. her body was numb but the pain medicine was beginning to wear off and the effects of the bullets were coming back.

Naomi was shot three times. One in the chest, one in the arm and once through her head. the head shot did the least damage beings though it was a graze. it knocked a section of her hair out and broke the skin but only chipped her skull. The .223 would've knocked her head off if it wasn't for the quick warning of Khalil.

"Well if I'm being honest, we aint got shit but about twenty thousand. Our kill rate receipt was blown to pieces with the car and you the Gov' don't do reprints so we assed out with that. There might be some cash at Cortez crib or even Pretty P's spot. You know Cordy ji-like moved himself in so I'm thinking I should go check them spots out."

Naomi wasn't pleased. she just knew that she was the one to kill Diamond and she was home free. The only good part about the situation was that Khalil was still alive so it was a win. After taking in the news she looked to Khalil, "So what now?"

"Well, like I said, I'm about to check Cordy and Pretty P's crib for some dough. We still gotta get the hell outta here."

"I'm coming too. I'm--"

"No you're not!" Ol' Man Harry interrupted, "You need to stay here so your stitches don't open back up and get infected. Khalil needs not go anywhere either but he hardheaded."

"Yup, Mr.. H! You know me so well. And on that note, I'm outta here," Khalil leaned over and kissed Naomi on her fore-head. "Ite, Ugly. Ill be back later, hopefully with some cash to get the fuck."

"Be safe Stink! Play your mirrors, okay."

"Yes, Mom, anything else?" Khalil said in a exaggerated tone.

"Get Out, Boy!" With that he was gone.

CHAPTER 30

Khalil

Came a long way from being a kid. Things and situations forced my youth to accelerate. Accelerate. That's a word I just learned and stop using it. But whatever. Living on the edge nowadays was regular; still Id never slip. Through the bullshit i had to remain real. it was either remain real alive or real dead and Id rather not be the latter.

Every since I got my first pistol all i did was slang it. If anybody wanted work I had the job for them. I was so messed up in the head that if the thought of drama would arise I was geeked to express it. I never backdown from no one, that was dead.

The Killzone opened man doors to violence which left no choice but to get with it or get lost. Sitting in he car I collected my thoughts. A couple weeks ago me and Naomi were on our way out of the Killzone. I blew a sigh, "Damn I hope it's still some cash in the crib." I said as I turned the ignition on the Caprice. Cortez was dead but his whip was very much alive and all mines.

The engine growled when it came to life. while Naomi was going through her rehab I made a few changes to the whip for my liking...oh yeah and safety. I didn't tell Naomi. She just would've been mad at me for spending the money.

I didn't do a lot, just a few minor tweaks. New wet paint, new motor, new feet, new guts and i couldn't forget some new beats. Got some armor around any and everything that could blow up and I definitely couldn't forget about the camera in the rearview either, 'YEA I SEE YOU' I smirked looking at the emptiness behind me through the visuals.

Made sure to do whatever it took to keep me and Naomi safe. the bullshit with Diamond was too close for comfort. some nights I feel like I had to get out the city. Putting the car in drive I pulled off in the direction of Cortez's crib. i cruised to a track that had my shoulders jumping. My window was slightly cracked, only enough so that a breeze could come through. The music that played had an effect on me. Had me ready to shoot and ready to kill.

Looking around I was actually looking for some smoke. Anybody could get it. The previous weeks played a heavy part in my actions. it was like a personal reality check. Aint no picks, no types, no nothing. Everybody as a potential confirmed kill.

Living this life of getting bodies and money had became my mission. It was time to get to the bag and keep my own vision straight for the border, to freedom.

Arriving I was cautious. carrying the 'glizzy' and a 'SD', there was nothing to talk about. Wasn't trying to hear no brother shit, homie shit, peace shit, woosah or nothing! His house looked empty and quiet but i wasn't stupid. Only a fool would accept that as facts. Anybody popped out, I wouldn't hesitate to put a hole in the ball team on their cap.

The door was unlocked. I pushed through and it made a creaking sound, "Shit!" I paused and held my breath with the

Glock in my hand. Didn't know why I held my breath like it was purposeful. My eyes wandered, silence lingered the air.

Advancing farther into the house the smell of weed still potent. Cortez's presence lingered in the area and it wouldn't leave me alone. The lost of him was an opened wound that didn't seem to heal. The pain of lost was just too real. i already knew that time wouldn't erase my big homie. Looking around different memories rushed my mental. In front of me was the living room where intense games were played and multiple woman were put to bed.

Naomi never knew the things me and Cortez would do. He introduced me to a whole new world when we were together. he literally held my hand through the years.

"And who the fuck are you?" A voice asked from behind me after I heard him chamber a round.

"Shit!" I lowered and shook my head, "Slim, I aint nobody. I was looking for my mans."

"I'm glad yo accepted the fact that you aint nobody!"

BOOM!

My body flew on the couch turning it over as the shot sent memories through my brain as if it was all over for me. the first thought was the rules. First rule: No loafin', which means no slipping. I was bullshitting reminiscing on past endeavors, and the bamma just shot me.

Luckily I had my trustee vest on. but the shotgun slug had my back hurting like shit as I rolled over for cover. "Hey Guy!" Th voice inched closer to me as I pulled myself up. "You dead yet?"

My Glock was dropped when I flew back and he knew that but what he didn't know was that I had my SD tucked on the small of my back. Made sure to be silent as I retrieved it. Unlike the Glock, the SD had a safe that I clicked off. One round was already in the chamber ready to attack his internal organs. I had a pretty good idea what he wanted to do to me so I had to beat him to the punch.

Seemed like confrontation wasn't anything new. Thanks to the government, it's the new normal. The guy tried to collect on my body either to leave here or just for his own guilty pleasure. Either way he wasn't getting neither one of them off today.

I heard him getting closer as he cautiously crept. He stepped on a piece of broken glass that gave away his position. quickly I stood and pointed my pistol squeezing at the large frame in front of me. he was slow on his reactions and the result left him lying on the floor surrounded in a pool of his own blood.

Standing over top of him i nudged him with my foot, "Hey Guy. You dead yet?" No acknowledgement came from him, pulled my phone out and snapped a picture with a thumbs up then sent it to waste management for pick up.

As I waited for my receipt and points to hit my account, I searched the house. Cortez's house looked like a bachelor pad. It had every game system, bongs, endless old DVD's, and candy dishes full of candy and condoms. The walls were painted pine green with marihuana patches through out.

Every room held something different. There was a shoe room, shirts and pants, draws and socks and even a hygiene room. The master bedroom was real freaky. the smell of funky sex was in the air and hit strong as soon as I entered. Instinctively my nose frowned.

'FUCK IS THAT SMELL?!'

Pointing both guns I searched the room and came up empty. I found the safe open with nothing but space inside it. Began to feel like the search was going to be a bust when I heard some moans coming from a closet. I raised both pistols. Really I wanted to just shoot through the door and deal with it when I opened the door but decided against it. I put the SD back on my hip and turned the knob to the door as I pointed, "Don't do nothing stupid. We ten deep so don't make us act a fuckin' fool, Homes." I bluffed.

Opening the door wide my eyes bubbled from the sight before me. There was one dead girl, that explained the smell, and a another one tied up crying. As I noticed the other girl, she looked familiar. I knew the girl. She went to school with me back in the day. I actually had a crush on her but she was way out my league.

I pulled the sock out her mouth along with the tape that covered it. The first thing she manage to get out vocally was, "Water." I looked around then shrugged. She still hadn't looked up at me as she spoke, "Please don't kill me. I'm nobody, please just let me go."

Cant lie. I was torn between the two. Kill her ass and get my points or let her go and hope she don't snake me out later. We had history. I use to cheat off her test, unknown to her. That count right. She probably don't even know or remember me. I looked at her before I spoke. I started with her name, "Teasha!" She looked up slowly as i continued, "Is that you?" Even though I knew it was her, i still had to play a role but her beauty was undeniable. She had a smile that only could had come from heaven.

"K-Khalil!?"

'OH SHIT! SHE REMEMBERS ME. OF COURSE SHRE REMEMBERS ME. IM THE FUCKIN' MAN.'

I use to always tell her that someday when the sky fell I would be right there to save her. I never knew it to be really true. But she didn't know that, cause there I was.

"Yup, it's me! Tol' you you'd need me one day." I said with a smile alittle to big showing my true feelings.

"Oh my God! I'm so happy it's you. I thought it was another rapist or murderer. Did you get both of them?" She asked as I untied her.

"Both of them?"

"Yea, it's two of them."

That put me on high alert as I looked around. But I was pretty sure I checked the whole house. She stood behind me still alittle shook up. "Khalil, can I have your other gun?" She pointed to my waist. She noticed the bulge on my back.

Giving it to her I kept walking. I didn't want any surprises but that would had made too much sense.

"Khalil."

"Yea," I turned around to face down the barrel of my own pistol, "Shit."

"I'm sorry, Khalil. But i cant keep getting tricked, used and abused by old friends. You don't know what I've been through. And the other guy that had hostage was friends with your sister and her friend. I'm tired of being the victim, Khalil!" Tears ran down her face, "Not any more! I'm not-"

"Wait, listen, Teash. You know me. I'm not them. You know we always been on good terms. Shid I damn near loved you from afar. I would never hurt you. Put the gun down. We in this together. I promise I wont ever let anyone hurt you okay. Just put it down."

I could see my words were working. Slowly she lowered the gun as I neared her. by the time I made it to her, the weapon was by her side and I pulled her into an embrace grabbing the gun. "It's okay, Boo, I got you now."

Rule #2: Remain emotionless. Another rule broken, but I didn't care. She was worth it. She was my unicorn. Rare and loyal.

Reluctantly she melted in my my embrace and agreed to come with me. Still I was confused about what she had said so I decided to ask, "So who was this other dude?"

"We need to hurry and leave before he comes back. If you killed the fat one, the other one is more violent. he never touched me but I've seen him do some crazy shit when he was off that P.c.p." She said as she tried to pull me to the door.

I stopped her and turned her around with a frown on my face. "Are you talking about, Tez?" Her eyes bubbled upon recognition of the name, "chill, chill. He dead. He got killed a couple weeks ago."

She let out a sigh, then continued to pull me. "We still have to go! Now it make sense because for the last few days Fat bastard been acting real crazy. Just earlier him and some other guys ran a train on the girl in the closet.

"She bit one of their dicks off and he shot her. They all ran off headed t some med guy in the hood with promises of me being next. So like I said, we have to go!"

Leaving the house I made sure to take in my surroundings. Teasha had said that the fat dude had friends and I wasn't trying to meet them. Quickly I helped Teasha in the car that sat 24 inches off the ground then I jumped in as well then raised all of the newly purchased bulletproof windows and hit the gas.

Looking around my mind wondered. It was a nice day other than the situation and living conditions. The summer was beginning to bloom. Hot as shit in other words. I had the a/c on "Crank!" The sweat beads on my head dried instantly. Outside was normal looking but dangerous. The toxicity was at an all time high from constant smoke and gunpower.

"Where are we going?" Teasha looked around as I drove.

"Gotta check another crib for something. Is there somewhere you want to go?"

"No," She said just above a whisper, "Just was asking."

I could tell she was still alittle shook from whatever she saw or went through. In time she'd heal. She didn't have a choice if she wanted to survive. She as always a quick learner and she had to had learned something if she was still alive.

"Hey Teash, do you know how to shoot gun?" It was a random question. I had to know though, especially is she planned on sticking around.

"Yes and no." She started,

'WHAT THE FUCK DO THAT MEAN?' My thoughts

"Well I know the general functions or what not but I'm no 'John Wick.'"

Her comment put a smile on my face. that was enough for me. If she stayed, i had the plan to teach her how to be a shooter, y'know, like me, Hitman. Cortez taught me that it's eat or get ate in the Killzone and I'd be damned if a wild dude swallowing me or mines.

"Oh ok, we'll work on that asap. If you want to survive this Killzone you gonna have to know more than just the functions. As you know, its crazy out here and aint no rules to this shit..."

As I drove and talked, I could feel her eyes staring through me. I could tell she was taking in all the information as if it was new news. That was good though. Needed her to absorb any and all information if we were going to be in the same space. After

I finished we arrived at Pretty P's spot where Cortez had been before his demise. I missed my man. he was definitely thugged out. All he ever known how to do was thug, hustle and kill a dude when he had to.

Khalil

Reaching into my waistband I handed Teasha the gun back. I kept the Glock for myself. No safety needed for me. Staring at the house I recalled my last visit there. It was some freak shit going on down in there. I couldn't bring myself back there and declined the multiple invites Tez had sent. My response was always the same, "hell nah, it's kids painted everywhere in here."

We walked to the door and a red laser shot out the peephole and I just knew it was over for me. But instead of bullets flying the dot turned into a line that stretched my body then began to scan me. I stayed still as it beeped, then chimed.

A sexy voice came through the intercom, "Scan complete, welcome to the pleasure factory, Khalil." Then the locks were disabled. I was in awe as the door auto matically opened and we walked in. Teasha gave me a look with side eyes. I don't know why but I felt the need to defend myself in that moment, "I don't know why that happened. This was my homies crib."

I didn't want her to feel no type of way about that. All she did was nod and walk past as she said, "Um hmmm."

Didn't really notice how nice the house really was last time I was there. There was a party going on then and a lot of decorations were in place. It was a colorful scene with different themes set up everywhere. With all the extra gone it looked like a nice place to live.

Teasha began to walk around with the gun at her side as if it was nothing, "Aye Teash, you need to have the gun pointed in the direction you're walking. Don't get all comfortable." I warned.

She looked over her shoulder at me. "Oh my fault. I thought you was this Hitman character so I should've been protected."

"Shots fired huh? You got that. But nah', on the real, somebody might be here like your ass was at the last spot."

"Tsts whatever," She up'd her SD, "Better?"

I didn't answer. I just walked ahead of her and continued to look around. I was on a mission. Had to find out if Cortez left a stash of cash for me and Naomi, if not we were back to the drawing board.

CHAPTER 31

Teasha

In the house I searched for anything of worth. Nothing specific, per Khalil but Im not dumb. I know he was in search of something though. I was just going to look for anything that could free me from the horrific life Id been forced to live. I'm not even a Washingtonian. Ima V.A girl that happened to get caught up in the shuffle. The worst thing I could had done was go out with my friend that night. They were calling it a "KILLZONE FINALE PARTY" A lot of people attended and I actually had a blast. One of the best parties I'd ever went to. I loved parties in the city back then. I had some good weed and slight drinks had the vibes mellow.

Then it happened.

Sirens went off as we were crossing the bridge. we all knew that the Killzone was to be in effect that night. At 11:59 pm we were on the bridge headed back to my Arlington home to chill for the rest of the night. Seconds later an explosion erupted instantly dropping the road in front for us into the river.

Almost simultaneously gunfire erupted around us. People were killing without cause. i was oblivious to the fact or the rules of the Killzone because I had no plans to participate. In front of me I watched in horror as people killed and then took pictures. Later I found out the reasons behind it.

Horrified, my friend and i ran back toward the District. we had no other options as bullets flew pass our heads ricocheting off other vehicles. I'd never been in a gun battle, let alone even heard or shot a gun.

I experienced a lot of first that day. Some still haunted me each day. Like when my friend was abruptly taken from me. Never will i forget it when the large caliber bullet struck and took half of her face. She was no angel by far but still she didn't deserve to go out like that.

Being though my family was across the bridge and i had no brothers to protect my honor or to even come look for me, I was stuck. Not to mention I didn't even have proof of my identity because i was using a fake id to get into the city. Stupid. But the walk to my fathers house was long and scary. I'd already enrolled in school the previous year using his address, I was studying to be a vet' since I had been working in a clinic and grew a love for animals. My "lift" or my friend would pick me up and take me back and forth to the safety of Virginias suburbs'.

In Virginia I was LaTeasha. But in the Killzone that name was non-existent. I was just Teasha, a brown skin bombshell. I stood 5'1 in a half, "Yes give me my half of inch", and curvaceous. Dark brown eyes and high cheek bones, courtesy of my Daddy. Every mans dream in my opinion.

Living in the Killzone changed me. crazy enough I didn't know if it was for the better or the worst. Still it was a constant fight between ying and yang. Perfect example, I was still wondering if i should actually knock off Khalil for my own bigger picture even after he rescued me.

Yeas he saved me. Yes he is sweet and i actually know him to be a cool guy but like I said, It's the Killzone we're talking about. He might have changed for the worst and playing me. I was always told that the eyes tell a story and his seemed like a movie filled with bloodshed and tears.

"Aye, Teasha! Where you at?" I heard Khalil call for me.

"I'm in here!" I yelled as I stuffed some jewelry I found in my bra, "I'm in the backroom!" Pawn shops still exist and I could get some money for the items.

"The hell you doing?" He asked, looking at me suspiously, "You look like a deer caught in headlights."

"I'm not doing anything!" I countered, "Did you find whatever you was looking for. I see you have a bag now." I said after noticing it hanging from his shoulder and trying to get the heat off me.

"Matter fact I did. I see you found something of interest too unless you got some lumpy ass titties." He nodded at my breast. "they looked good earlier now they looking crazy. You got at least some double D's and yes I was looking."

For your information my girls are 40D with one D thank you and keep your eyes off them!" I rolled my eyes and walked past him.

"My bad, 'cuse me." He said to my back.

Seeing he still had his boyish sense of humor I decided I wouldn't try to back door him...at least for now. Still I wondered what was in the bag, i figured if it was of any importance I'd find out later.

In all actuality I was so tired of being in the city. I missed my family, mainly my granny. They probably thought I was dead. Multiple feelings attacked me daily. All i did was think, think, and think so more. Suppressed by all my childish fears, I had to act hard when I really was scared. Id been through a lot before the Killzone and it just prepared me for the new battle.

I remember dark skies and lightning all around me. Each flash was etched in my mind, it seemed as if the sky was about to burn. I just knew it was a sign from above and the reaper had finally found me.

All I could do as the gunfight went on was hide in a vacant car and try to wait it out. Multiple explosions were near me that had me frightened that i might blow next. After a while it was silent. Coming out of the car it was as if nothing was left and the city was abandoned. Looking to the sky, all that fell was debris which was thick ashes that felt like snow.

"Let me drive?" I asked as he tossed the bag in his trunk. he burst out laughing at me like I said the funniest joke in the world. Not going to lie, I felt some type of way about that, "Never-mind!" I rolled my eyes and jumped in the passenger seat then crossed my arms.

"Awww, look at the big baby, "He teased after getting in the car, "You can drive next time in a safer area so you aint gotta sit there poutin'." He said turning the ignition.

"You aint-" I was cut off by the oud music as the car came to life.

He tapped his ears letting me know he couldn't hear me then started bouncing his shoulders to the beat and pulled off, "Asshole." I said but knew he couldn't hear me as I leaned back.

Really I wanted him to stop by my aunt's house so I could grab some things but I knew it wasn't safe. that was how I got kidnapped in the first place doing just that. I've learned not to cherish any luxuries because in the new world order of the district, everything comes and goes.

Even the life that i was given was borrowed because we're not promised a tomorrow. A lot of people living their lives as if it's going to be their last and I didn't blame them. but I'm not going to break. I knew there would be better days if I could just get the hell out of The Killzone. And my best chance in the moment was with Khalil.

CHAPTER 32

Naomi

Slowly, drifting slowly. The pills had my head spinning like a bottle cap. But I knew it was time to get up and get out. Ol' man Harry and his wife had been great but I couldn't stay there. They needed to worry about protecting themselves, not me.

The bounty was probably still on my head. I've done things before I wasn't the blame. Definitely didn't deserve what Diamond caused. Lately my parents had been on my mind, they stayed in my head and really couldn't understand why. But since they left my world it seemed like the sun didn't shine as bright. Hadn't really been myself, then the scare with Khalil really messed me up. I know them feelings couldn't had been good for my health. But there i was climbing out the bed trying to leave. Soon as i made it to the door it opened.

"What you doing out of bed, Sweetheart?" The elderly lady asked attempting to block the door. Her eyes were scanning me as if I was in the wrong or something. I didn't like her aura, something wasn't right.

"I'm fine, miss," I paused expecting her to fill in the blank of her name but she didn't, "Miss lady I guess, but I have to leave. I don't want to bring ya'll any trouble. people are looking for me." I confessed.

The lady had to be at least 65 years of age but she didn't age well. Her years aged her badly so when she gave me a smirk before brandishing her weapon which was a nine millimeter Smith and Wesson, I was confused.

In a creepy witch like voice she said, "Yeesss. I heard there is a pretty penny on your head. It's more than enough to set me free. I'm not trying to live my last days in this God forsaken Killzone mess. Harry must be crazy still defending that gate. he can stay, but I'm cashing out." She raised the gun.

"Wait! Please, the person who put the price on my head is dead. You wont even get paid." I reasoned.

"Now Chile, you know that's a lie. Any and all hits must be accounted for before the hit goes live. her death only made your contract open forever."

"So you mean to tell me that you nursed me back to health just to kill me?" I genuinely wanted to know. It made no sense to me. She could had killed me the second Khalil left, and him for that matter.

"That's whats wrongs with you kids today. You don't read the rules or instructions to anything. When the bill was passed it specifically stated in order to get paid for a kill, you must be the sole person to commit the murder. As you know, you had multiple holes in you that was given by someone else. All life threatening damage must be carried out by one person. You're all healed now which makes it possible for me to collect the benefits." She chambered a round.

The day was full of surprises. Never had I'd known that in order to receive credit you had to be the sole killer. No co-defendants. My heart dropped at the sound of the gun becoming ready to collect. I closed my eyes ready to accept my fate.

"Lorretta! What are you doing, Baby?" Ol' man Harry walked in and dropped the bags he was carrying.

"Stay out this, Harry. I need the money. I cant continue to live like this. Day after day we continue to help people, for what! Pennies on the dollar. No! I'm done. This is the last one. the biggest payout. You with me or not?" She turned the gun to him. Her hand not certain as it shook but her eyes told a different story.

It looked as if Ol' Man harry was actually contemplating the option. I took that second to bull rush the woman who I learned was Lorretta. We crashed into the wall. she was old but not small. the gun and slid. My eyes followed it. before i could make my attempt toward it, a sharp pain attacked my face. Lorretta struck me!

I could taste the blood in my mouth as another fist hit me. Covering my face her assault was constant as i balled up trying to find an opening to strike. And there it was.

That Ol' Bitch wanted problems so I had to solve them. I grabbed her thinning ponytail and pulled myself so I was on top of her. I had a hand full of hair and with other hand, her head became my speedbag as my circular punches shot at rapid fire.

Completely forgetting her age I fought like we were on the school yard and she tried to play me. The threat on my life was real. She wanted to dance with my hands so I gave her the full wraft of my rage as her face beat up my hands.

Ol' man Harry tried to pull me off but a quick jab to his aging balls sent him straight to the ground. I felt like they both tried to violate. I crawled to the handguns quickly as possible and turned it on the both of them when I had a hold of it.

Standing tall but pointing the gun down I spit blood on the floor. "So this was the big plan huh? You was going to nurse me back to life then kill me, huh?" I turned the gun on Lorretta, "You gonna go first you ol' Bitch! I fuckin' hate-"

There was a presence, "What's up, Nay?" Khalil asked in the doorway with some chick.

BOC!

I shot Lorretta in her head before Khalil tried to talk me out of it. His eyes bubbled as I turned the gun on Ol' Man Harry. The chick with Khalil took cover behind him as I put three holes in Harry and two more in Lorretta for good measure.

"Damn, Nay. Fuck happened to you? I know that Ol ass woman didn't beat your ass?" He giggled.

"Shut up! You got your phone?"

"Yeah, why? Ion' need you all on my feed with no bullshit." He said as he strolled down his Instagram account.

"No Stupid, take the pictures for waste management."

"Oh okay. I got you."

Craziest thing ever, social media was now available for the people inside the Killzone. At one time it was restricted. Now we could keep up with the Kardashian. The world was moving normally while we were on pins and needles for their personal pleasure, gain and enjoyment.

Khalil took the pictures as I started at the chick who looked familiar but I couldn't place her. Khalil had so many female acquaintances that I didn't know if she was a Killzone whore or a genuine friend of his. She must had felt the vibes because after a second or so she spoke, "How you doing, Naomi? It's impolite to stare." She said with alittle too much attitude for my liking.

"It's impolite to do a lot of things nowadays. It's all about what you going to do when someone does it." I fired right back and stepped forward.

"Whoa whoa whoa," Khalil jumped in-between us. "That's not even bouta' happen." he looked at the girl. "You. Chill," Then me, "Sis. Chill." I rolled my eyes.

'CHICK TRIED IT.'

Had to respect the girls gangster. Even though I had a gun in my hand she didn't back down. It wasn't pointed at her or anything but still. I'm a firm believer, thanks to Cortez, that if you raise your gun at somebody you better kill them.

She stepped in front of Khalil directly in front of me. I looked her up and down, gun still in my hand. She smiled then stuck her hand out, "Hey Naomi, I'm Teasha. Your knucklehead brother and I went to school together."

Putting the gun on the small of my back I extended my hand to accept her truce. Just like that any animosity was squashed. Still I wondered why she was there, but knew Khalil would tell me eventually. Releasing Teasha's hand I gave my attention to my brother.

"So.." I talked with my eyes.

"Good, but not sooo good, " He said referring to our money. I blew a sigh, wanted to know more but didn't want to put Teasha all in our mix. she seemed cool but shid, Diamond was beyond cool and everyone knew how that cookie crumbled, "But we gotta get outta here. Im sure somebody heard them shots and you don't have a vest on. We gotta go check on the crib." Khalil said.

Beings though Ol' Man harry and Lorretta were deceased, I didn't hesitate with my suggestion to clean the house of everything. Surprisingly Teasha was the first to grab a bag and start to fill it up with medical supplies. The girl had beauty and brains. That gave her a few points in my book.

Khalil went straight for the armory. he'd known that Ol'man harry had an arsenal of weapons. He was the gate keeper, so I knew his selections were plentiful. When I thought things couldn't get any worst it happened...

Never had we heard the siren go off since the initial start of legislation. The loud sound forced us all to stop what we were doing and look at one another. Khalil was sliding up and down his phone as his eyes bubbled, I was nervous as I asked, "What is it, Stink?"

"Shit crazy! My news feed goin' bananas right now from the outside of the killzone. they talking about some new rules that's going to change everything! we gotta go outside so we can hear it."

"Hear what?" He wasn't making any sense to me.

"The announcement about to broadcast for the whole city to hear it."

Headed to the door we all chambered a round as we opened it. shockingly so many people were already on their porches wondering and waiting for the news to be announced.

The siren stopped and a voice chimed in:

'ATTENTION! ATTENTION! ALL RESIDENTS PRSIDING IN THE KILLZONE PLEASE LISTEN AND UNDERSTAND. ANY AND ALL KILLS BROADCASTED ON 'LIVE' WILL BE DOUBLED. THE ORIGINAL 150 BECOMES 300, THE 100 INTO 200 BUT THE 10 WILL REMAIN THE SAME. THANK YOU FOR MAKING AMERICA GREAT AGAIN, EFFECTIVE IMMEDIATLY'

"Aint that a bitch." Khalil sigh and shook his head.

There was complete silence on the block as it seemed if everyone were processing the new information. i never knew that, that many people even still lived in the neighborhood let alone the block. The silence lasted all but fifteen seconds before the first shot rang out.

"Get down!"

Teasha and I ran back in the house for safety. Khalil, "HITMAN' like a crazed assassin ran toward the fight firing his gun from the porch. He actually became a good shot and people were falling because of his bullets. Screaming his name I tried to get his attention. He was in a zone as he fired multiple shots. I knew what would grab his attention.

"Daddy said to take care of me, remember! Not get killed!"

I noticed his shoulder dropped in defeat as he lowered his gun and rushed inside where we'd wait it out. Teasha looked at Khalil as he walked past, "You a knucklehead. Who the hell do you think you are? The terminator or somebody. You gotta got yourself killed." Her face was balled up.

He looked over his shoulder, "Something like him, but I'm better." He blew the barrel of his gun. I blew a sigh and closed the door.

Didn't know what I was going to do with that boy. Things were changing fast and rumors of new rules to come flooded social media. hoped it wasn't true but with my luck, Every single rumor would become a fact. Sometimes I wished I could've tied them in our shoes. When I say them, i meant everyone participating in the genocide by choice, masking it as gentrification.

Sitting in the living room the shots were continuous as we listened. Teasha and I were chilling as i turned on the tv. Al she wanted to watch was the damn ID channel. Khalil kept pacing back and forth as he glanced out the window here and there.

"Stink! Stay out the window!" I yelled when i noticed him. He looked me up and down then frowned his lips before he said, "No! That's why your ass look like you look now. Keep thinking shit don't stink. You talking about some wait it out. Fuck dat! We need them kills to get the fuck outta here, Nay!"

"First of all, watch your mouth when talking to me! You need to get out of that you against the world bullshit. We're in this together so you need to act like it. Plus it looks as if you have a plus one to look after as well."

Teasha stood up, "Oh no, Boo. I don't need your brother to look after me, no shade, but I'm straight."

Khalil giggled at her comment, "Girl you know damn well you need me to keep you safe and warm at night." He smirked.

"Boy bye." Teasha rolled her eyes and sat back on the couch watching reruns of Snapped.

"Bye nothing! That's what;s wrong with your ass now! Keep watchin' that crazy ass shit on tv."

"You scared or something? You want me to snap on your ass." She smiled a devilish grin.

They were flirting with each other like I couldn't read between the lines. It was cute. I hadn't seen Khalil googly over a girl since before all this mess started. Still I wasn't trying to hear it. "Hey! Hey! Listen. Ya'll can do whatever this is later but right now we need to be quiet before we draw too much attention. " I lowered my voice with each word.

Khalil looked at me crazy then said, "Mannnm fuck them! I got a gun, you got a gun, she got a gun; fuck we hiding for? The car right there in the driveway and it's somewhat bulletproof."

"Somewhat!?" Teasha cut her eyes at him.

"We ite! Don't even trip, Boo, " He winked at her then looked at me, "We need to be in the field, not laying around waiting to get shot. My vote is to leave and get our plan together at our own safe haven, not this Ol' ass house that aint even protected. So what's up, Nay?"

Naomi

'HMPH' I blew a sigh. He was right. Ol' Man Harry's house wasn't really safe compared to our home and with the changes in the rules we couldn't stay here that long. I reluctantly agreed. "Ok Stink, what's the plan?"

CHAPTER 34

Khalil

"Bout time you started listening. I am kind of awesome or what not."

Teasha rolled her eyes. "Boy."

"Just saying."

Really I didn't even have a plan. But staying in this bullshit of a house was not it. I wondered how Ol' Man Harry stayed alive so long. Then again the more I thought of it, I knew. He was a vicious hoarder. He had guns galore. he probably could had paid for his exit ticket by selling all his spinventory one by one. Honestly I knew a lot of people like him. Cortez was one of them. the love for the city kept them in the Nations Capital. I loved my city too but shid', soon as I get the funds I was out of there.

Originally from the block I was always ambitious even though I came from the trenches of northwest's slums. My mind was always on the bigger picture. Never really accepted the word "cant" They had to explain to me why I couldn't have it. The hunger in me evolved during the killzone.

"Stink! Hello?"

"What?"

"Your plan? Teasha and I waiting to hear this extravagant plan of yours." Naomi said with a little too much animation for me. I waved that shit off.

"I'll tell the both of you once we get to the crib, capeesh, so get locked and loaded. We headed to the whip."

Peeking out the window I wished I was myself. It's easier to watch your own back than yours and multiple people. there were so many unclaimed kills just laid out. I wanted to claim them as mines, but then again if the kills was broadcast on 'LIVE' there wasn't a reason to take the picture.

"How do it look out there, Khalil?" Teasha asked as she gathered her belongings which was my gun and a purse.

"Regular. You know, bodies in shit everywhere. It really looked like GTA out here. But ya'll ready?"

Opening the door I didn't wait for a response. They knew what time it was and what had to be done. The car was close. Probably a hop skip and a jump and we'd be at the door. Pressing my key chain, the V8 engine came to life. The sound of it turned a few heads and I let off some cover fire so Naomi and Teasha cold make it to the car.

The first shot gave the neighbor a new eye socket as he tried to aim his phone and the gun at the same time. That shit was a set up in a gun fight when the shots were coming from multiple angles. I dropped about six people as I made it to the car. "Damn" I said getting in the car.

"What, Boo, I mean Khalil." Teasha tried to clean it up but I knew she was feeling me but playing hard to get. I acted like I didn't even hear her.

"What!? What you mean? You aint see all that sharp shooting I just did. I deserve a fuckin',award since I cant claim them kills without getting killled." I said putting the car in drive plummeting over multiple bodies as I drove. The car sat high off the road that the bodies had no effect on the under carriage as the shocks made it feel like we were on a boat, smooth sailing.

Turning the corner all the fireworks were left in the rearview as everyone in the car shoulders dropped with relief. The sky was gloomy. Looked like all the smoke from multiple rounds in different area placed a dim glow over the city.

Shots could be heard from all around which made me put the pedal to the floor as the trunk dropped and front rose while the tires spun.

"SLOW DOWN, STINK!"

"FOR WHAT?" It made no sense to me. No laws. No police. No restriction. No need to mention that random people were shooting at us. But no! Naomi wanted me to slow down. I ignored her as I fishtailed a left down a one way.

"Stink!" Naomi was pissed.

"Ok, damn." I eased off the petal as Teasha hit me in the back of my head forcing my neck to cringe.

"Stupid. What's wrong with you?" She asked disgusted by my actions.

Didn't understand the flack I was receiving. All the good guy tried to do was get us safely to the crib. We were only a few blocks away but in that short distance I could've easily counted thirty bodies . The new law had family turning the other cheek and looking out for self.

Driving I even saw fist fights and stabbings among other things. All involving people who were neighbors for years and vowed to protect each other in the beginning. It could only get worst because there was more to come. Before getting in the car my news feed was going crazy from the rumors. Usually when something from the outside of the zone was trending it would soon be a fact inside of the zone.

They were the ones voting on what happened inside of the city as it was. Knowing that always kept me on edge. About a block from the house I saw a childhood friend running, well sprinting. So many shots were being fired I never thought they were aimed at him as he ducked and dodged. In his hand was a de-cocked pistol.

No bullets.

I pulled beside him, "Get in, Bruh!" He looked with wild eyes as he still tried to run. The calm finally hit him when he noticed I was a friend.

"K-Khalil?! Is that you?"

"Yea, Fool, get in!"

He reached for the door with urgency. No sooner than when he grabbed the handle, his head exploded dropping him instantly. "Shit!" I gassed the car the final block until I pulled into my driveway. Naomi didn't give me any bullshit about speeding that time after she witnessed homeboy head hit the window in brain matter spurts.

Opening the first gate I looked around and ran to the door to insert the code unlocking the door. Pushing the door wide I looked out to the street with my pistol aimed at anything and everything, "Come ya'll, Hurry up!"

Sitting in the living room inhaling the potent intoxicant my mind wondered. 'HOW WE GONNA MAKE THIS MONEY?' We really were at the bottom, the rock bottom. Really had to come up with the money or live in the Killzone until we were killed. The latter was never an option.

Seemed like we all were suffering under the crescent. and it will be a longtime before anything changed. But I refused to lose. I made a promise to my father to look out for my sister and apart of that promise was to get her to safety. Hot water wont be able to remove the blood from my shoes when I'm done with this City.

The Government done took everything but my soul from me. Couldn't let them get that. Not an option. "Can I hit that?" Teasha asked reaching for my blunt.

I pulled it out of reach, "When you start smoking?" From what I remembered she never even thought of flicking a lighter so asking to smoke my blunt was foreign. She always liked the rough dudes but didn't like to indulge in the activities they were in. She was quiet and sneaky, like most Aquarius's but she did have hands', meaning she could fight. When 2chainz called himself the hair weave killer he must aint met her because after every fight her opponents hair no longer was attached.

"I started when that damn bridge collapse and i was stranded in DC and didn't want no parts of it. Is that reason enough?"

"Works for me." I gave her the blunt. Really I didn't want to. The blunt be the highlight of most days. In the Killzone there are usually sad days filled with lost and emotional reality. But me, I had to stay strong for more than myself.

Teasha looked at me as if she didn't plan on leaving anytime soon. "So what we gonna do now?" she asked as she inhaled. "What you going to do is puff puff and pass." I reached.

"Tst, I know that, Stupid! I mean with this new situation in the air. It was already dangerous, now it's like 'they' tryna speed the process of killing us."

Thinking about her statement, she wasn't lying. he illusion was that they were helping us by giving us more kill options with a higher payout but in reality the risk for points gave a higher kill rate for them. If you get killed and you was, lets say uhh, ten dollars from earning your asylum, your money gets forfeited.

You cant even pass your earnings off to no more. They get to keep all the money. Teasha had a valid point. If we wanted to survive we had to become more slick, more viscous and more dangerous. No one was taking prisoners. Shoot or get shot. That's the only plan at the moment. Honestly I hoped Naomi had a better option. Mine would probably result in a wrongful death. I said wrongful death because no one in my circle of loved ones are supposed to die. We're bionic! Everyone else is expendable in my mind. That was my story and I'm sticking to it.

Teasha continued to stare. I aint have any answers I was just rolling with the punches as they came. Shit, everyone was, "Khalil! Did you hear me?"

"Yea hol' on. I'm thinking." Didn't anything come to mind except that damn State farm commercial replying in my head..."I'm Jake...from State farm. It was catchy, kind of was mad that i knew it by heart.

The look I was receiving, one would had thought I had all the answers but wouldn't share them. Still I inhaled then exhaled the smoke in hopes of an idea. Looked up, was thinking. Nothing. I turned to Naomi who had been quiet since we came in the house for her opinion. Usually she always had a lot to say. "Nay!" She was lost in her own mind. She was physically there but mentally she was stressed. "Earth to Earthlings! " I blew a cloud of smoke in her face that grabbed her attention.

"What you say, Stink?" She fanned the smoke.

"I aint say shit, but Teasha asked what's the plan? Leave it to me it's gonna be mission after mission until we get the bag and blow this city, but I know you probably have a more logic plan."

"I-I don't know." She sounded defeated.

CHAPTER 35

Teasha

WOW! I might've been better off by my damn self. Seemed as if the two of them didn't have a clue to the next move. I could do bad all by lonesome. The effects of the marijuana had me thinking. 'WHAT HAS BECOME OF MY LIFE?' I had been victimized and couldn't even blame it on police brutality. They wont even pull up. Everyone treating people as a victim of hate. Really I hate to see that the government rather see us dead and gone instead of helping us.

Walking through the halls of their Georgetown "estate", I was shocked and impressed. Never in a million years would I had thought Khalil was living like that. Maybe it was a Killzone home that was bought for cheap.

'YEA, HAS TO BE.'

Back in school he wasn't living like that. Everything now was damn near new and polished. One would think they had a butler. Entering a room, don't know who's, I laid on the bed eagle style and stretched out. I was exhausted. It was a long day and rest was needed. My eyes began to drift as I stared at the back of my eyelids...

There was a time in life when I used to look into my fathers eyes and felt safe. In a happy home, I was his princess and he held me on a golden throne. Unfortunately them days were gone but the memories still play vividly in my head. My ears wiggled as I heard the songs from different places in time. There I was walking across the golden sand of the beach, then a loud bang!

BOOM boom!

Shots!

I jumped from the bed and crept to the door. Didn't know what was going on. All that was confirmed was the shots were fired. the next task was to find out if the shots were deadly and if the friendly fire had come from a team member or the ops'. Coming into the hall there was an eerie silence that I didn't like.

Silence usually meant death. Creeping down the stairs I remained vigilant. the house seemed bigger than ten minutes ago as I cautiously looked around. I made it to the living room and the scene before me made me gasp, "Oh my God! Cortez, I thought you were dead!"

A Sneak Peek

COMING SOON

BLUEFACE DREAMS

THE PROLOGUE

The police lit 'em up with their lights. "What's up, Dro?" Black asked. "Want me to take them on a ride?"

Dro inhaled a big breath, then exhaled. "Pull over." They looked at him like he was crazy. It was something in his eyes that made Black comply. Truck in park. The officers pulled behind them. "I ain't goin' to jail, Slim," Dro said, looking forward. "Mask down."

Everyone in the truck pulled their masks down in compliance to Dro's orders. "Kill 'em."

The officers never seen it coming. The windows was tinted five percent. Four doors flew open. Dro was geeking, ready to put in work. It was all or nothing. He had a new STAG 8T.

He was trying to see what that gas-operated piston action was about. He lifted the rifle, looked through the diamond head premium flip-up sight set and squeezed . . .

TAT TAT TAT TAT . . .

Dro fired the assault rifle in semi-automatic spurts, connecting with the first officer's body. His mid-section looked like a Picaso painting as his shirt oozed blood.

After the first shot was heard, Izzo dived on the ground. The bullets felt like they were flying too close for comfort.

"This nigga crazy!" Izzo shouted.

Dro was shooting, approaching the squad car as endless shells hit the pavement. BOC! BOC! BOC! Black fired at the other officer as he jumped over Jroc who was laid out on the ground, not used to the sound of choppa bullets.

The police never had a chance to draw their weapons as their bodies spread on the street, one sliding down the car slowly.

Dro shot so many shots that the car began to flame. Slowly, Jroc and Izzo stood up and looked at each other through the truck's window with wild eyes. Black and Dro walked to the corpse for good measure and fired.

BOC!

TAT! TAT!

"I'll drive this time," Dro stated with his hands out awaiting the keys . . .

CHAPTER 1

"What's understood, don't need to be explained," said Dro.

It wasn't your average night in the city. Washington, D.C. that is, the only place in this country of ours that should be called the city, Our Nation's Capital.

Rain descended from the dark clouds as Black and Izzo crouched behind a car waiting on the right moment to strike. Black didn't mind the wet pavement; it actually was to his advantage. Izzo on the other hand was beyond pissed as a car cruised, splashing water as it passed.

"Shit! My sneaks!"

"Shhhh nigga," Black hushed him.

Moves and quick come ups was daily routine for Black. Nothing he did was for fun. There was always a reason behind his raft. Today he decided to bring along one of his best friends who didn't mind doing anything for the sake of a dollar.

It was closing time at the corner store the Ahab owned. Salim, he was a young, but balding foreigner that was talking real greasy and slick to Black earlier in the day disrespecting his sister and all the while hiding behind the protection of the thick window divider.

That action alone was what triggered Black to make him pay. In a high-pitched tone of irritation Izzo complained. "Damn slim, you got me out here in the fuckin' rain messing up my fit and I just got my dreads retwisted."

"Shut up, nigga, nobody told you to look all sexy for a robbery."

"All you said was come on and I came."

"Shhh . . ., there he go."

Coming out the creases Black sprung up to make his presence known. No mask or nothing, he wasn't worried about his face being exposed, this was personal. Frozen in place, Salim raised his arms to the sky in surrender. In broken English and a heavy Arabian accent, he pleaded, "Please . . . no harm . . . all to take yours," he said trying to pass off some pocket change as he stared down the barrel of a loaded handgun that Black pointed.

Izzo was still behind a parked car a few cars back trying to get his ski mask out his side pocket. The rain made his pants stick to his skin a little too close for comfort.

"Stupid ass skinny jeans," he cursed himself.

Finally getting the mask out his side pocket and over his face he got up to assist Black but heard a siren in close vicinity. He ducked back down, hiding from the sound by looking around trying to locate its physical presence. Salim heard the siren as well, as if he was a cartoon a light bulb shined bright over his head. He had an idea and wasn't going to let that opening he had close. "Oh Allah! Thank you, the police!!" In his native tongue he lied and to his surprise it worked.

Black turned around with lightning speed, nervous and scared he would get caught. Looking around he didn't see any sign of the police. Turning his attention back to his victim, he seen the Arab sprinting down the street as water splashed with every stride he took. "Shit! . . . bitch ass nigga," Black murmured as he began to give chase. Izzo looked up and over the car he was ducked behind to see the Arab running his way.

"Uh uh nigga, I got your ass." He tiptoed to the sidewalk and stuck his leg out in an attempt to clip Salim up. The power from Salim's stride forced Izzo to fall as the Arab fell and rolled a few times a couple feet forward. Black was on Salim's heels until he ran into Izzo as Salim got back up continuing to run.

"Move nigga! Get out the damn way!" Black said running over Izzo.

"Ahhhh shit! Get dat' nigga . . . damn, fucked up my whole leg!" Izzo whined getting back up trying to run through the pain.

Salim was pretty fast. He moved through the parked cars and traffic with ease and agility. Onlookers and passersby looked on in awe of the chase. No one really cared for the Arab, so no help was in his near future, at least not from the residents in the area. He was considered an asshole to most. He'd put tax on top of tax basically robbed the lower class but catered to the high class. The chase was intense. Zig-zagging block to block, Black kept up with his pace, but couldn't gain on him. Izzo was tired, Newport's and good weed had him winded. His leg was pulsating with pain which was another deterrent slowing him down. Izzo leaned on a light pole trying to catch his breath.

"I'm right behind you bruh', get that nigga!" Looking left then right, Izzo spotted a motor scooter approaching. "Bingo." As if he was a Major League Pitcher, he whined back a hay-maker punch. CRACK! That was the sound of the connection from fist to chin as the rider flew off the scooter.

"Can I ride?" Izzo asked picking the bike off the ground. Chucking the deuces to the fallen rider, he rode down the street to catch up with Black. Salim was running for his life determined not to get caught by Black. He knew Black was crazy, now he was regretting all them wolf tickets he been selling behind the safety of the plexiglass. Black was getting exhausted. Out the corner of his eye Izzo came flying past him. "Come on, slim, speed up." Izzo smirked. Izzo was on the Arab's trail gaining on him by the second. Pulling on the right side of him he kept his hand on the throttle. "Hey buddy, you okay?"

"No!" Salim responded still running but pointing behind. "Call police! Mad man robs me." Izzo cruised beside him. He tried to throw a left hook. In his mind he thought it was gonna be a for sure knockout punch, swinging the punch he boasted, "They call me Floyd!" The hit connected with the back of Salim's head with little to no damage.

"Ahhh! Oh no." Salim reacted instantly turning off the street through an alley. Izzo tried to grab him but ran into the car in front of him that stopped for the red light. Black caught up with Izzo as he was trying to get the scooter off himself.

"Floyd my ass. What kind of punch was that?" he said as he cut through the same alley following Salim.

"Fuck . . . you . . . nigga!" Izzo cursed at Black's back. ". . . Blackass got me out here chasin' a nigga in da rain . . . in skinnies."

Izzo cut through the same alley to see Salim done trapped himself off. "Ok, slim," Izzo said to Black, "looks like Obama ain't the only nigga to catch a Bin Laden lookin' muthafucka, huh?" Black was heaving with his hand in his thighs and his gun resting on his knee. "Like I was saying before you decided to think you were Usain Bolt, where dat' shit at?"

Salim looked around and noticed he was caught. "Here." He tossed a velvet zip lock pouch with today's date. Flipping through the content, a smile spread across Black's face, then tossed it to Izzo. Izzo fired up a stogy and looked himself over. He was disappointed at what he seen.

"Look . . . at . . . this . . . shit . . . here," he said referring to his outfit.

Izzo reached for his gun that was tucked in front of his briefs, "I'ma kill em'!" Black laughed as he watched Izzo struggle.

"Nigga you can't even get that muthafucka' out them lil ass jeans you got on." His gun was still trained on Salim as he spoke.

Dipping and swatting Izzo was determined to free his weapon, "Hold on, Moe . . . I got his bad ass."

"Please don't kill me!" Salim pleaded.

"I wouldn't be Black if I didn't, Slim."

Boc! Boc! Boc!

Black shot Salim all in his upper torso. Finally getting his gun freed from his waist Izzo pushed Black out the way, "Move, Fool, I got em'!"

POW!

"Thank you, come again." Salim was silenced with the final headshot.

"Really, Dude, all that work for that lil ass p-shooter," Black said clowning Izzo's gun as Izzo blew his smokin' barrel.

"Who's bad?' Izzo imitated Michael Jackson.

Running out the alley the coast was clear. Sirens was nearing the car Izzo hit with the scooter was bringing unwanted attention. The doors were wide open with no driver and a blaring horn." We gotta dip!" Black stated. They weren't too far from their neighborhood and that was the next location they needed to be, in order to be safe.

The rainy weather turned into a storm as the traffic lights began to flicker yellow. The neighborhood had a leery silence as if everyone knew a life had just been taken. Making it to the courtyard of the housing projects of Lincoln Westmorland Izzo noticed his building was fogged out, nothing was visible from the outside looking in. Climbing the few steps to enter the building it had no locks or keypads. It was always broke. Izzo just opened it to a cloud of smoke attacking his nostrils.

"Damn, who got it?" Izzo asked as he noticed his two other comrades.

Dro and Jroc was sitting on the stairs smoking the building out. These four together was unstoppable. As kids they made a pack to remain loyal and always keep it 100% with each other. Friends from the sandbox, nothing or no one would come between them. "I should have known it was you two niggas," Black said coming through the door behind Izzo. Izzo tossed Black the pouch from the earlier caper, and they split it down the middle. Fifteen hundred dollars a piece was what the lick brung. Dro shook his head at their transaction, "I see y'all on that bullshit today, huh?"

"The grind don't stop, Baby!" Black said fanning the crisp twenty-dollar bills in the air. Izzo looked toward Dro and Jroc and asked, "What y'all doing in my building anyway?"

"We knocked on your door, but from the looks of things you niggas weren't home, now were you? Next thing I know is that it started pouring down out there so naturally your hallways became the layover, ya' dig." Jroc answered.

Thunder roared. The sky was lightening up. It looked as if fireworks were in the clouds. Everyone was on their own level as the blunt circulated in the hallway of the building. Laughs and loud conversation had the neighbors opening and closing their doors to make a statement. No one cared or responded, couldn't anybody tell them nothing, as far as they were concerned this was their building.

The night was still young in most eyes, it was only quarter to nine. Everybody was smacked, meaning they were high out their mind as they exited the building. "Next spot after body drops, the muthafuckin' liquor spot!" Black said as Dro shook his head reading between the lines of that statement.

"Don't be trippin' in shit when we get this bottle either" Dro told him.

"He a'ight we a'ight. We got each other, right?" Izzo said grabbing Bro and Black into a huddle while Jroc laughed rolling another spliff.

"What's understood, don't need to be explained," Dro stamped.

A Sneak Peek

✦ 199 ✦

COMING SOON

EXPOSURE

PROLOGUE

Don

It was November 29th, a few days before the Thanksgiving holiday that was quickly nearing. Don, a nineteen-year-old high school drop, from the Forestville county of Maryland was casually strolling down the aisle of a Costco Superstore in Alexandria, Virginia to purchase last minute items to complete the upcoming feast.

In his ear was a pair of "beats" he listened to, bopping his head as he checked the labels and sale prices off the list given to him by his girlfriend, Natasha. They had been exclusively involved since the young adolescent years of junior high school and were still going strong even though the older they became the more different their lifestyles became.

Whereas Natasha was finishing her first degree in medicine and Don was selling poison on the street corners. He also held a part-time job doing construction. His main focus was taking care of his little brother Travis. A few years ago, the brothers suffered a loss of their parents to a violent, meaningless accident which left them parentless and turned into an instant father at the age of sixteen. The foster care system wasn't an option. His only option was the streets, and he went headfirst.

Oblivious to his surroundings, Don shopped, tossing different items into his cart until a shadow towered over him in a sweeping motion that caught his attention. He turned his attention to the bold man that slightly touched him as he passed. A face of recognition triggered in his brain. "Corey?!" He hadn't seen this guy since school about three years prior, "Is that you?"

The teen looked when hearing his name but didn't stop in a usual gesture and speak. His arm continued to sweep as a whole shelf of Ramen noodles landed in his cart. "Don? What's up, Man! Long time, but what the hell you shopping for? You better grab that shit and go, you must ain't been outside?"

Don narrowed his eyes. "What the hell you talking' 'bout? I'm not bout to start stealing, especially not 'round here."

Corey went to the other shelf, "Look around you, Brah! It's the end of the fuckin world! People eatin' people in shit! I'm outta here, nice knowin' you, Homie."

Corey slid another shelf into his cart, but this was canned goods then continued down the aisle dragging two carts.

Don pulled his ear buds out his ear and really began to pay attention as he looked around. It was Pandemonium! People were running every which way doing the same thing Corey did. Taking everything! There was a gunshot! Reflexes forced Don to a crouch as he began to duck walk to the end of the aisle to see what was going on. The security was shooting people recklessly. "WHAT THE FUCK!" Don panicked looking both ways in search of another exit than the one in front of him. If the security would shoot unarmed white people with no remorse, Don knew for sure that he would be targeted. It was all of thirty seconds when the shooting stopped, and Don peeked over a register. The security guard was not visible, but the surrounding scene was a violent one. As Don eased to the exit doors with cautious steps in attempt to leave, the security guard stood up with his ear and eye socket eaten out with blood running down his face. Don froze in place with bubbled eyes shocked as the security guard remaining eye found focus on him. The security guard yelled a horrific moan and ran toward him. Don pushed a cart in front of him, "FUCK NO! Is that a zombie . . ."

CHAPTER 1

Israel Eskow – November 19th

It was the end of his last period class for the end of the day at George Washington University and Israel Eskow, a wealthy biochemist and part-time chemistry professor at the university couldn't wait for his students to exit as he dismissed the class. "Hurry, hurry now! I have things to do!"

As the last of the students exited the class, he locked the door and slid the curtain on the door closed. Heading to the back of the class he went to a cabinet and spun the combination until the lock opened. Cautiously he began to pull out the materials that he stole from the CDC where he worked for his personal project. Hell bent on vengeance, he mixed a few dangerous biocides that he planned on injecting into Peter McCalister, the dean of students.

Behind Israel's back he was the laughingstock of the college thanks to this man, Peter, who had been sleeping with his wife and was caught by a student on multiple occasions receiving oral in the office and the act was captured on video. It spread through the students and eventually made it to his phone. The video had him outraged!

The once quiet, smart, and well accomplished scientist deteriorated day by day from the pain and finally had his breaking point when he was invited to a Thanksgiving football party then encouraged to bring his wife to it.

"Don't you come without her, okay?" Peter had said a couple days ago with a wink.

Today he had the final biohazard that would hopefully alter the cerebral Cortez and dumbfound its host. When it's all complete, his wife of ten years would only have eyes for him. Israel Eskow stood a mere five feet four inches and was thin as a rail with a receding hairline, whereas his wife stood at five feet nine inches easily towering over the man in height and beauty.

Stacey Eskow was white, auburn hair with bright green eyes and long legs with an ample rear end. Clearly, she was out of his league. Blinded by love, Israel was unaware that it was clearly greed on those green eyes of hers and the only reason she loved was his account balance.

Israel placed his bio suit on to protect himself from infection as he mixed the hazardous chemicals watching them bubble, transforming different colors. Carefully he inserted the syringe and filled it to its max as a devilish grin spread across his face.

Completing the task at hand took the whole lunch hour. As the bell rang, he unlocked his class to exit. He didn't have any afternoon classes. The halls were flooded quickly as students returned to class from their lunch break.

"Mr. E, what's happenin'?" a student asked as he walked by.

He gave a quick wave, "Hello, young man," and never broke stride. He was on a mission. Peter was going to become an instant case and have down syndrome at its highest level and also carry hepatitis A-Z and whatever else from the deadly viruses that leaked out the syringe in his lab coat.

Standing in front of a door that had a label right above his head that read "DEAN OF STUDENTS," he swallowed the lump that felt like a jawbreaker in his throat as he knocked two slight taps at the door with his keys.

"Come in," a voice called from the closed door that Israel knew belonged to Peter. He blew a sign and outstretched his fingers, wrapping them around the knob to enter.

The autumn sun attacked his eyes as Peter spoke, "Mr. Eskow." He stood from his desk coming around to lean on the front of it extending his arm.

"What do I owe the pleasure?" Peter was six feet tall, white with an athletic build that could be seen through his suit. He played football in high school and college. He was for sure to get drafted by the NFL, but a career ending injury changed his lifestyle. Inside his office was the memory of the "glory days." Multiple trophies and awards were on the shelves with a shine as if Peter just dusted them off. On his desk was a family portrait of his average wife and two kids. The sight of the kids almost changed his mind.

"Hello, Mr. McCalister—"

"Just, Pete, buddy."

"Very well, Pete. About your invite. I have to respectfully decline the gesture. I hope you understand."

Peter squinched his eyes, cocking his head as if he was confused. "Don't be silly. I've spoken to Stacey and everything is a go." He patted Israel on his back forcing his body to flinch from the touch as he began walking to the door about to open it. Israel seen red.

The fact that Peter had the audacity to admit to he'd spoken to his wife, had private conversations without him knowing and was on first name basis was the confirmation he needed. As Peter reached for the door, Israel pulled the syringe from his coat pocket and jammed it into the neck of Peter.

"Hey! What the hell is this?" Peter screamed pulling the empty syringe out of his neck, instantly becoming groggy.

Israel smiled. "See if you be getting your cock sucked now when that kicks in . . ."

CHAPTER 2

Taylor Nicole

"So where are you spending your holiday?" Taylor asked her friend Sonya as they sat in class.

Taylor, a student at Georgetown on her way to completing her major in criminal justice was smiling ear to ear listening to her friend gossip about everything but the question she asked. Taylor is white, skinny, but petite with big breasts that most thought were fake because of her size, which was five foot six with red hair.

Her parents are wealthy and made sure that her education was paid in full. Taylor had dreams to be an FBI, CIA or any type of agent like her grandfather. The stories he told to her as a child sunk unto her brain and put the passion of the shield in her heart.

She could handle most weapons with ease and couldn't wait to be an agent and protect and serve. Taylor had an apartment on campus, but still visited home every weekend to her family's home in Woodbridge, Virginia. Not because she wanted to, but because it was part of the agreement set by her father.

"Sonya! Did you hear me?" Taylor asked Sonya who abruptly stopped talking to look at the door with bubbled eyes.

Sonya put a finger up, silencing Taylor before her rant began. She wasn't the only one staring in the direction of the door, the whole class was. The silence in the class turned everyone's attention to each other as curiosity arose. "What's going on out there?"

"I don't know. Somebody might be playing a prank or something. These guys are so stuck in high school, like come on, right?"

"No, Taylor, those are screams." Panic could be heard in her voice as she stood sliding the chair from behind her forcing it to fall.

Taylor was already on her feet and jogged to the door. Her eyes widened. "Oh my God!" She quickly ducked and slid down the door then reached to turn the lock. "Everybody be quiet!"

The teacher stopped his lecture finally turning around to face the class. "Ms. Nicole, you will not be disrupting the—"

"Shhh!" Taylor put a finger to her lip and whispered, "Something is out there and it's eating people."

"WHAT!!" Zach, another student, stood and ran to the door to get a visual for himself. "No way, let me see! He was excited as he pushed Taylor to the floor out of the way from the door. Zach peeked through the tall slim glass and noticed students running for what looked like their life.

"Oh shit! She ain't lying." He watched until a body came crashing violently on the door getting attacked. The dead body slid down the locked door revealing the culprit. The once janitor stared through the window at Zach.

He ducked quick. "Shit, shit, shit! I think it seen me."

The teacher approached. "What do you mean, 'It'?" then grabbed the lock turning it. "Don't be silly. Calm down class. I'm going to get to the bottom of this." He turned the knob, never looking out as the door flew open. "AHHHHH!!!!"

The janitor latched on the neck of the teacher and begun chewing away at his flesh. Taylor grabbed Sonya and ran past as Zach was next to get grabbed by both the teacher and janitor. A few students made it out, the rest weren't as fortunate.

Hand in hand, Taylor and Sonya ran down the halls blending in with the chaotic crows in an attempt to make their exit as well. Sonya had another girl's hand, but quickly released it as she was dragged down by a bitten student.

There was pandemonium everywhere. Pushing through the double doors of the building they made it outside. It was a bloodbath. Everywhere they looked someone was running from an attack. Multiple students laid dead on the pavement, most of their body gone and decomposing rapidly.

Taylor froze in place after really seeing all that was before her. Sonya tried pulling her, but the sight before her froze her as well. They were mannequins. In Sonya's eyes were her boyfriend of two years eating another student and drop him and then run for another that crossed his sights.

Taylor, a natural protector took a step toward a wounded victim that held her neck crying, but abruptly stopped. The victim began to twitch as her body jerked, snapping bones in and out of place. It stopped. It looked around, death in its eyes. "Come on, Taylor! We have to go."

This time there was no hesitation as she ran with Sonya to her car. Inside the car she waited for it to come to life as she tapped her foot nervously and impatiently. Directly in front of her was another one of her friends running, but she was tackled and then bit. The corpse laid dead as she watched to view that in seconds the body began to twitch. Fifteen seconds! She counted before it rose with a thirst for blood.

"Yes!" Sonya screamed as the car finally turned over on her old model Toyota. Putting the car into gear she left the scene plummeting over a few former friends that were no longer the same.

QUESTIONS FOR DISCUSSION

In the prologue how does Naomi's actions set the tone for her new reality?

How does Naomi's parents' death help shape the relationship with Khalil?

Did the Kill zone change Naomi for the better or worse?

Was Diamond's treachery transparent from the beginning?

What examples can you list of when Diamond made decisions based on emotion rather than logic? How did those decisions work out for her at the time?

When Khalil looked to the sky and said, "I told you I got her Dad." Did you think it was over for him?

How does Naomi's relationship with Diamond change from the time the bill was introduced until the end of the book? Are there any clues in the story to predict its outcome?

Was Cortez' death expected and deserved or surprising and disappointing? Explain.

How does Diamond justify her actions? Does Diamond truly believe it when she tells herself that Naomi always wins and now it's her turn? Was it jealousy or envy or both that motivated her actions?

What emotions did Naomi feel after the death of Cortez? Did it build more anger toward Diamond? Was Cortez' death expected?

Was Khalil's death a shocker? Did you expect him to make it? Do you think he's dead for certain?

In the end, does Naomi live happily ever after, after all she's been through? Or should she return and reek havoc on the Kill zone for vengeance?

Author's Note

A common question asked to me is "What are you doing in there?" I kind of have a smart mouth so instinctively I want to say, "Time!" When you get sentenced over 200 months in a federal prison you tend to lose the patience for "dumb questions," but in all actuality it's not a dumb question. For a longtime I would say, "I'm just doing this mutherfucker." Now that was a dumb answer. When all your talents are on the outside of the gate what do you do? Easy. Something new. I love reading and I have a wild imagination and I started to feel like I could do this too. Write a book that is. What better way to take my mind outside of my environment than to get lost in a story. The first thing I did was start reading a lot, different genres. Sometimes a book a day. Getting the feeling of how different authors express themselves was my way of hands-on experience. So that was my first progression, just reading and getting familiar. Next step was to put the pen to paper, crazy enough I'm my worst critic. Friends will tell you anything, some tell you the truth. But in the end, I received more thumbs up than down and felt it was time for the world to feel my words and it was time to share. So, if you like this book, get ready for a line of good reads coming your way. I love feedback so don't hesitate to reach out. I will hit back.

ABOUT THE AUTHOR

C. C. Spicer is crazy about writing. He has a wild imagination where he paints words and captures the reader's attention. He places you in the story. Writing wasn't always a passion of his growing up in the Nation's Capital. Life in the city wasn't an easy task. The pressures of urban conditions swayed him to the streets where he fell victim to one bad decision that changed his life. Twenty seconds instantly turned into twenty years. This is where he found the love for the pen and changed his life, dropping the sword. He'd love to hear from you. Send your questions or comments directly to him.

Mail:
Cedric Spicer 40847-007
F.C.C. Petersburg
P.O. Box 1000
Petersburg, VA 23804
E-mail:
spicer_cedric@yahoo.com
instagram@dro_pak2.0